"Did your uncle talk to you, Mickey?"

The little girl nodded. "Yeah—the big lecture. Now I know the phone number, the place where he works ... and not to go with strangers." She grinned at Deanna. "Are you a weirdo?"

Deanna grinned back. "What do you think?"

"Nah. But Uncle Lee said I should have been more careful. That you could have been a witch or something, and I'm lucky you didn't bake me in your oven or steal me away on your broom." She giggled. "I told him you're too pretty to be a witch."

"Thanks, kid," Deanna said dryly, wondering what her neighbor's response to that remark had been. "So—are you getting another baby-sitter?"

"I guess." Mickey glanced sidelong at Deanna. "It would be nice if I could just come over here and have you look after me."

Deanna repressed a shudder. Mickey was an adorable child, but that uncle of hers ... *Infuriating* was the only word for that man!

Samantha Day, a Canadian author, started work on her first novel—a futuristic story, complete with romantic hero and heroine—when she was fourteen years old. Having long perfected the art of daydreaming, she now shares her fantasies with a devoted readership and makes romance writing her full-time occupation.

Books by Samantha Day

THE THREE OF US
OF US
Samantha Day

Harlequin Books

**TORONTO • NEW YORK • LONDON
AMSTERDAM • PARIS • SYDNEY • HAMBURG
STOCKHOLM • ATHENS • TOKYO • MILAN
MADRID • WARSAW • BUDAPEST • AUCKLAND**

ISBN 0-373-03297-8

THE THREE OF US

Copyright © 1994 by Samantha Day.

Printed in U.S.A.

CHAPTER ONE

SUMMER HEAT LINGERED long after the sun had set. The air was close and humid as though a cooling storm approached, but no wind stirred the trees and the sky was clear of clouds. A faint sprinkling of stars could be seen through the glaze of city lights.

Fitfully Deanna Hamilton tried to hold on to sleep and to her dreams, but heat penetrated with cloying reality and her eyes opened. Remnants of dreams hung for a moment in the dark corners of the room, then dulled and faded as she awakened fully.

She sat up and leaned her head on her knees, sighing softly. A glance at her bedside table showed Ryan's picture, details muted in the dimness. Pieces of her dreams flitted through her mind, briefly vivid. Ryan, alive again, healthy, happy, loving her...wanting her.

Slowly she got out of bed and went to stand beside the window. She lifted heavy, sweat-dampened hair from her neck and knelt on the hardwood floor, resting her elbows on the sill. Through the trees, she caught a glimpse of the pool in the neighboring yard, streetlights glinting on still, cool water.

A sudden longing to feel that water close over her heated body caused her eyes to widen, and she wondered if she dared. Chances were nobody would ever know. Her new neighbor was rarely home and she had seen no sign of him for several days. It would be wonderful to swim, to let the cooling water drain her of this restless, dream-stirred energy.

Deanna tapped a finger against the sill in indecision. It probably wasn't a wise thing to do, but it was tempting. And who would know? *Go for it,* she told herself, standing up. She went to her dresser and rummaged through the top drawer for her bathing suit.

Quietly she slipped outside, followed by two half-grown black cats that instantly blended into the shadows of the night. She walked quickly over the lawn to the old stone wall separating the two properties. There was a bench resting next to it, under the spreading branches of a crab-apple tree. Standing on the bench, she peered into the neighboring yard. As expected, it was empty, and no lights shone from the closed windows of the house.

"Well," she murmured, "here goes." She pulled herself up and swung first one, then another, long, bare leg over the top of the wall. She sat for a moment looking around.

She felt cooler now that she was out of the house, and wondered if maybe she shouldn't just go back inside and content herself with another shower. But she had come this far, and the smooth, glinting water beckoned. She stretched her foot until it touched the cedar railing of the deck that ran from the house to the pool. With a lithe twist and jump, she was on the deck, brushing bits of mortar from the palms of her hands, and in another moment, had slid soundlessly into the pool.

After a couple of quiet laps she turned onto her back, moving her arms languidly to keep afloat. Her hair trailed behind her, slow currents giving it a subtle life of its own. The water was silkily cool and refreshing.

She gazed into the sky, thinking about her dreams, recalling their essence, but none of the detail. Tonight there had been a physical longing for Ryan, a memory of their lovemaking. It was natural, she supposed. It was so long since she'd been loved.

Sighing, she kicked her legs and started to swim again. Water churned as memories chased her—the last weekend away with Ryan before their world had collapsed, snowbound at a ski resort in Quebec, holed up in their chalet reveling in their isolation and each other, carefree and passionately happy.

With a groan, Deanna dove beneath the surface, driving away the sting of tears. She swam until her lungs could bear no more, then burst to the surface again, gasping. She clung to the side of the pool, resting her head on her arms for a moment. She was cool now, and tired, yearnings and painful memories buried once again. Sleep should come easily.

Wiping the water from her face, she looked up. A man stood there, just back from the edge of the pool, almost directly in front of her.

Heart jumping with fright, she pushed away and stared at him, her eyes wide and startled.

He took a quick step forward, light and shadow rippling across his lean, muscled body. He was wearing nothing but brief nylon shorts, and his face was dark and without expression.

"Who...who are you?" Deanna's voice rose with fear, sounding unnaturally loud in the still night air. She inched closer to the shallow end of the pool.

"Who are *you?*" he demanded, his words thick with anger. "And what the hell are you doing in my pool? Get out."

Jaw thrust forward, aggression showing in his stance, he watched impatiently as she climbed out on the opposite side.

Her apprehension mingled with sharp embarrassment, and Deanna walked quickly toward the wall, leaving a glistening trail of water behind her.

"Sorry," she murmured, with a glance over her shoulder. "It won't happen again."

From what she could see of his face, her apology didn't appease. His expression was cold and hard, and as he made a move she felt a little knot of fear twist in her stomach. He was angry, and he looked strong enough to be threatening. She hurried to the wall.

Just as she began to hoist herself up, the outside lights came on. She peeked back.

He stood with his hand on the light switch, scowling as he watched her ungainly effort to scramble over the wall.

"If you're thinking about repeating this little performance, don't. Next time it's the police."

She had no doubt he meant it. He was eyeing her closely and she had a sudden, discomforting picture of how she must look pasted against the wall under the harsh glare of the yard lights. The stone tugged at the bottom of her bathing suit and water dripped as she swung her legs over the top. She glanced at him again.

He was right below her now, standing with his hands on his hips, broad shoulders back and legs apart. His eyes, dark in the shadows of his face, moved slowly over her. Deanna shivered. His lips curled in a tight, taunting smile.

"Better run while you can," he said, the words a growl.

Deanna needed no further warning. Turning quickly, she launched herself into her own yard. She felt the stone scrape roughly along one thigh, and she landed heavily on the grass, cursing softly in pain. Picking herself up, she limped to the back door. As she opened it, she heard his low, mocking laughter join with the nighttime sounds. Shivering again, she slipped inside, finding the laughter somehow more disquieting than his anger. She locked the door behind her.

Deanna paced the floor, berating herself for even thinking of trying to sneak a midnight swim. Embarrassment was only a part of what she was feeling. She would have expected annoyance on her neighbor's part, but his reactions had gone beyond that. He had been very angry, and something in his stance, in his laughter, had left her feeling threatened.

Normally she might have considered waiting until morning, then going to apologize. But not with this man. She would stay well out of his way.

So much for getting to know her new neighbor, she thought with a grimace, then shrugged. The whole incident was best put out of mind.

She was too restless to go back to bed. Instead, she changed into a short cotton robe and went to sit at the kitchen table, a stack of loose-leaf paper in front of her. She doodled absently, trying to keep her thoughts on what she had written the day before. But she kept seeing how she must have appeared to her neighbor, pinned against the wall under the glare of the yard lights, her bathing suit riding low as she scrambled to the safety of her own yard. She could hear his mocking laughter as clearly as if he stood outside her window. It was enough to make her cringe all over again.

With effort, she forced her attention to her work and began to read what she'd written. It took a few minutes, but eventually she was able to slip from the real world into one of her own invention. Frowning in concentration, she made some quick changes then, after a thoughtful moment, began to write.

It was much later when a scratching at the door brought her head up. Blinking rapidly, she pushed the papers to one side and stood, stretching stiffened limbs and yawning. She opened the door. The two black kittens scampered in and headed straight for the food dish in the corner of the room.

"Hi, guys," Deanna said, shutting the door. "Have a nice night on the tiles?" She opened a cupboard and took out a box of cat food, adding a generous amount to what was left in the bowl. Within seconds of hearing the dry food rattle against the sides of the box, another, older cat trotted into the kitchen. He stopped and glared balefully at Deanna before continuing to the food.

She laughed at his obvious dislike of the kittens. "Get used to it, Leo," she said as he pushed his grizzled gray head between the two sleek black ones. "They're here to stay."

When they'd finished eating, she let the old tom out while the two black ones sat washing themselves. Flicking off the light, she went up to her room and straight to bed, refusing to give in to the urge to glance out the window at the house next door. She was more than ready to forget the whole, uncomfortable incident.

Morning started much too early with a phone call from someone offering her a special deal on carpet cleaning. After refusing with as much politeness as she could muster, Deanna hung up. She hated sales calls.

Flopping onto her pillow, she debated going back to sleep, but decided it would be nice to get a jump start on the day. She had some errands to run, and if she got them over with in the morning, she would have the afternoon to write.

A quick look outside showed a powdery blue, cloudless sky. It was already warm and promising to be hot, a typical prairie summer day. Deanna showered, then dressed in khaki shorts and a black tank top. She ran a pick through her wet hair in an attempt to tame the curls springing into life as they dried. Giving up, she tossed the pick onto the dresser and went downstairs.

While coffee brewed, she pulled the night cover from a bird cage hanging near the kitchen window. Two blue budgies danced along their perch in noisy excitement.

"Cool it, you two," Deanna murmured. "I'm not ready for such enthusiasm."

She poured herself a cup of coffee and sat at the table. As she sipped, she eyed the papers piled in front of her, thinking about the last scene she'd written. New ideas came to mind, and she grabbed a pen. She was still scribbling furiously when there was a loud knock on the back door. Startled, she inadvertently tipped over her mug, splashing coffee onto the papers.

"Damn!" Jumping up, Deanna snatched a tea towel and dabbed at the liquid. A quick glance assured her that her words were still legible.

The knock came again, louder and more insistent. Frowning, Deanna went to answer.

A man stood there, tall, handsome—and irate. Green-flecked hazel eyes were narrowed and flashing with anger.

Uh-oh, Deanna thought, and gripped the doorknob more tightly. She recognized him from the night before—dressed this time maybe, but every bit as angry. Now what?

"There's a gray cat behind the back wheels of my car. It obviously doesn't want to move." He held up a hand to show four reddening scratches running from knuckle to wrist. Carmine drops speckled the cuff of the white dress shirt showing beneath the sleeve of his suit jacket. "Is it yours?" he demanded.

Great, just great, she thought with an inward groan. Of course it was Leo. He was old and inclined to be cantankerous, but why did he have to pick on this man?

Her neighbor frowned impatiently. "Well?"

"Uh, yes, it could be mine. I'll go take a look."

He glanced at his watch. "Could you be quick about it? I'm late as it is, and at this point I really don't care if I run over the beast or not."

Deanna stared at him in horror. "You wouldn't dare!"

He laughed then, the same low, mocking laugh she'd heard following her through the sultry night. "Just get the damned cat, will you? I've got to change." He turned and strode down the sidewalk and out of the yard.

Muttering under her breath, Deanna went into the back lane.

It was Leo all right, sitting haughtily against the rear wheel of a low-slung sports car. The gleaming black hood was liberally spotted with dusty paw prints.

Deanna crouched down and snapped her fingers. "C'mon, Leo, old puss. Let's go."

Amber eyes blinked in her direction, then closed. He wasn't moving.

"Come on, Leo," she pleaded. "Let's go before he makes hamburger out of you." She knelt gingerly on the crushed gravel, reaching for the cat. He edged away.

Cursing softly, she wriggled under the car, closing a hand over the scruff of his neck. "Gotcha. Come on, you mangy beast. Let's get out of here before he's back."

"Too late."

Deanna groaned in frustration and backed her way out, bringing a reluctant cat with her. She scrambled to her feet, flushed with both effort and embarrassment.

The amusement on his face didn't help. She knew how she must have looked, half-sprawled under his car, rear end up in the air, and she cringed. As if last night hadn't been bad enough! She held the squirming cat tighter and glared at her neighbor.

"You didn't have to make such a fuss," she said defiantly. "If you'd just started your engine, he would have run off."

"After seeing the mess he made on my paint job, I wasn't sure I could stop myself from putting the car into gear and flattening him." He glanced at his watch and gave his head an impatient shake. "I'm late. Keep that animal away from my car. Next time, it's the pound."

He pushed past her and got into his car. As he moved hastily off to the side, he started the engine with a roar and backed quickly into the lane.

"I hope he gets a speeding ticket," Deanna said angrily. "It'd serve him right." She looked down at the cat in her arms and made a face.

"Thanks a lot, Leo. I really needed to run into him again. Stay away from him, please!"

Once securely behind her gate, she released the cat and went into the house.

After pouring herself a fresh cup of coffee, she sat down at the table, scowling as she thought about this latest encounter with her neighbor.

Before last night she had planned to go over eventually and introduce herself—she had been friendly with the previous owners and felt it was a good way to continue. She could forget about such niceties now. Two meetings, two confrontations. She didn't need any more of his high-handed arrogance.

SATURDAY WAS ANOTHER hot day. Deanna spent the morning working at her part-time job in a flower shop, then hurried home for an afternoon of writing, happy for the free time. The following week promised to be busy, and her book was at a crucial point. She scribbled furiously until early evening.

Finally she tossed her pen down and stood up to stretch. She went to stand in the kitchen doorway, rubbing at a kink in her neck as she looked outside. The sun had begun its slow decline, but the heat, she knew, would linger long after it had set.

She thought briefly about a cooling shower, then decided to do a bit of yard work first. The lawn should have been cut days ago, and it would feel good to do something physical.

She put on old, laceless runners and fastened her Walkman to the waistband of her shorts. Popping in a tape and placing the headphones over her ears, she went out to the little toolshed in the back corner of the yard.

It took several pulls of the cord to get the lawn mower going, but it finally started with a roar and a puff of blue-gray smoke. Deanna grimaced at the noise and turned up the music.

She pushed the machine across the yard, nodding to the beat coming over the headphones. Occasionally she made unconscious movements in time to the music. She breathed deeply, enjoying the smell of newly mown grass.

A sudden tap on her shoulder startled her. Mouth open and hand to her throat, she whirled around, but the movement threw her off balance and she fell onto her side. Looking up over crisp white slacks and a navy short-sleeved shirt, she met the flashing, hazel-green eyes of her neighbor. Fists jammed in his pockets, he stood above her, a derisive smile curling his mouth.

"What the hell are you doing here?" she snapped. How dared he sneak up on her like that! She scrambled to her feet, yanking the headphones from her ears and grabbing for the mower that had continued on a couple of feet under its own momentum. She turned it off. The silence was deafening.

She glared at the man. "Well?" she demanded tightly.

"Don't you think this is rather petty?" he asked coolly, ignoring her anger.

Deanna scowled at him in confusion. "What are you talking about?"

"This waiting until I had company to start mowing your lawn. We hadn't been outside five minutes when you started. It's pretty obvious you're trying to get back at me."

Deanna stared at him in indignation. She started to speak, stopped, then started again. "That's not true! How am I supposed to know whether you've got company or not? My lawn needed cutting and I was cutting it. That's all!" She glared at him, hating to be accused of such childish behavior.

"And if it *was* bothering you," she went on, "all you had to do was signal over the wall or something, not sneak up and grab me like . . . like some demented mugger!"

"I tried," he said, his voice dripping with sarcasm. "But you were plugged into your Walkman and gyrating around the yard like you were auditioning for a rock video."

He shook his head. "Look, I've got business to attend to. You can cut this some other time, can't you?" Without waiting for an answer, he turned and walked away.

Deanna stared at his retreating back, seething with anger. "Yeah, I can," she muttered. "First thing tomorrow morning, and I'll start right under your bedroom window!"

Damn the man! She hadn't seen hide nor hair of him since he'd moved in, and now it seemed as though every time she turned around, he was there, bristling with rude arrogance, taking offense over nothing. Three times in less than a week. It was too much.

For a moment she was tempted to start the mower up again and continue to cut the lawn, but common sense prevailed. She didn't want him thinking he was right, that she had started mowing the lawn just to spite him. Muttering, she tugged the machine back to the shed and put it away, then returned to the house to shower.

Afterward, she stood at her bedroom window, absently toweling her hair dry as she looked next door. He had company all right. Three men and two women sat with him on the deck. They seemed intent on the business at hand—an open briefcase lay on a patio table, papers ruffled by a breeze.

Deanna pressed a little closer to the glass, peering down on her neighbor. What kind of business was he in? And what was so important that he had to hold a meeting this late on a Saturday?

She stopped her thoughts with a shrug. Who really cared? But still she lingered and watched, until his head shot up suddenly and he stared in the direction of the window.

Deanna stepped back quickly. He couldn't have seen her, could he? Surely not. The last thing she needed was for him to storm over and accuse her of spying.

She wadded up her towel and tossed it toward the doorway to pick up later. Instead of working tonight, she'd go for a walk, maybe along the Assiniboine River to the Forks, and get something to eat at the market. She wasn't going to waste any more time thinking about her neighbor.

That was easier said than done. There was something about the guy that made it hard to put him out of mind.

DEANNA STOOD just inside her neighbor's yard, hardly believing she was there. An old woven basket filled with an assortment of tools was slung over one shoulder. At her feet was a folded stepladder and a bucket holding a wallpaper tray.

The call had come the day before from a woman looking for someone to paper a room. Deanna had come highly recommended from a friend of a friend. Would she do it?

Deanna had accepted with alacrity. She needed the money. It was only when she wrote down the address that her doubts began. It was her street and the number was just off by two. It couldn't be, could it?

It was. She sighed and shifted the basket from one shoulder to the other. This shouldn't be that much of a surprise. She'd papered rooms in several houses and condos in the district, getting the jobs through word of mouth. She was fast and competent, and many people seemed to prefer having a woman come into their homes.

She'd been tempted to call back and say she'd changed her mind, but she really wasn't in a position to turn down work. And it was strictly business, after all.

Resolutely she picked up her supplies and marched to the door.

A woman with a young baby asleep in her arms answered the bell almost immediately. There was an air of distraction about her, but she smiled warmly enough.

"Oh, good, you're here. Come in."

Deanna stepped inside the cool, tiled foyer. So he was married, and with a baby, to boot. It was odd she hadn't seen them around, not even coming and going.

She smiled her wide and friendly smile. "I'm Deanna Hamilton."

"I'm Sybil. Let me show you the room Lee wants done. I don't mean to be rude, but I'm in a bit of a rush," she added over her shoulder as she hurried down the hall. "I forgot I had to take Davy to the pediatrician this morning."

She entered a large, well-lighted room, followed by Deanna.

Deanna put down her supplies and took a quick look around. Straight walls with flat paint. It looked easy enough.

"This is Lee's den," Sybil said. She rubbed her cheek against her baby's head and flashed a smile at Deanna. "I told him I'd give him a hand with the decorating when he moved here, but once the baby came, I just didn't have the time. I thought the least I could do was bring him wallpaper samples to choose from and find someone to do the work. The paper is over there," she said, pointing to the rolls stacked under the window. "It was on order for weeks—I thought it'd never get here. Do you think it'll take you long?"

"I don't expect so," Deanna said. "What wall did you want me to do?"

"The one behind the desk and the one with the windows. Will you need any help with the furniture?"

There were only two black leather chairs and a cherry-wood desk with a computer on it. "I can manage."

"Good." Sybil sighed. "I told Lee I'd stay, but I've got to get Davy to the doctor. He gets his first shot today," she added, holding the baby closer. "I know I'm being silly, but it really bothers me. I hate needles. I usually end up half fainting. I can't imagine what I'm going to do when they stick one in Davy." She made a face and grinned sheepishly.

"I told Rick he'd better meet me at the doctor's office. I just hope he doesn't get too involved in something at work and forget about us. Lee's supposed to remind him, but he's just as bad, and they're really busy right now."

Deanna was slowly getting the picture. "You mean, this isn't your house?"

Sybil looked surprised, then laughed suddenly. "Me married to Lee? Goodness no! He and my husband work together, but we've all been friends for a long time, since university. Anyway, I've really got to be going. Do you have everything you need?"

"All but the water," Deanna said.

"The kitchen's thataway, and there're some cold drinks in the fridge. Help yourself. Oh, I nearly forgot. Your check is on the desk, in case I'm not back by the time you finish. I've got a few other things to do while I'm in town, but I should be through by mid-afternoon," she added on her way to the door.

This was all very trusting of her, Deanna thought, a little amused by the woman. She certainly seemed nice, though, even if she was just a little flighty.

"And the, uh, owner. Is he expected home?" Deanna asked. She sincerely hoped not.

"Knowing Lee, he'll be at the office until this evening sometime. It's nothing but work, work, work with him." Sybil rolled her eyes and shook her head. "Anyway, if you do leave before I get back, just make sure the door is locked, okay? Gotta go. 'Bye.''

"'Bye,'' Deanna echoed, then sighed, her shoulders slumping. Here she was, alone in *his* house. She would have to get the job done quickly—to say nothing of perfectly—before he got home. That way, he might never know she was the one who had done it. Somehow she was sure that if he did know, he'd find something to complain about.

She started by unplugging the computer and pushing the desk into the center of the room. She knew nothing about computers and hoped she hadn't inadvertently erased something, but the cord was in the way and she couldn't paper the wall around it. She laid a drop cloth on the thick, charcoal-gray carpet and made a quick trip to the kitchen for a pail of water. Once everything had been readied, she opened the first roll of paper.

The color and design were a shock. Tiny mauve fish, complete with miniature bubbles, swam through horizontal strands of twisting kelp of a deeper purple. Ugly was the only word to describe it.

"This is it?" she said. Surely the man had more taste than that. It might have done in a bathroom—might—but in a den? She really didn't think so. Still, it wouldn't be the first time she'd papered a wall with something she considered completely inappropriate. Everyone had different taste, and it wasn't her place to question their choices.

She let the paper curl back around the roll and opened another. It was exactly the same. They all were. She checked the bag they had come in and found the receipt. The code number matched that on the back of the rolls. It had to be the right stuff. With a shrug, she got to work.

"I just hope it doesn't make me seasick," she murmured as she hung the plumb line and began to measure.

The job went quickly. As always when she was working on mundane tasks, her mind was on her writing, and as new ideas came she would take a moment to jot them on a notepad she kept handy.

She wished she didn't have to take on odd jobs to supplement the part-time salary she received from working at the florist's. When she'd left her position with an advertising firm the year before, she'd hoped to have plenty of time for writing. Unfortunately some unexpected repairs on the house had made quite a hole in her savings account, and she had to make money wherever she could.

One published children's book and the sale of a second had not made her wealthy. She was working on the third of a series, hoping that her young readers would demand more of the same. A release in the States, or in Europe, was possible, but it was all so long in coming. Still, at least her first book was selling well. Bigger things should come in time.

When the last strip had been hung, Deanna stepped back to take a look. She groaned and shook her head. The result was hideous. The room positively swam with little purple fishes. She hoped it would make her irascible neighbor as nauseated as she was beginning to feel.

She cleaned up quickly, then took a final look, noticing the end of one strip didn't fit cleanly into the ceiling seam. She climbed up onto her stepladder and, with the utility knife, carefully worked the edge into place.

"What the hell is going on in here!"

Startled by the loud angry words, Deanna's foot slipped on the ladder. She fell against the wall, managing to regain her balance, but the knife dropped from her fingers and bounced against the corner of the desk, leaving a nick in the glossy wood.

Heart thudding, Deanna turned and looked down into the angry eyes of her neighbor.

They widened in recognition, then narrowed angrily. "You! What are you doing in my house?"

"Papering your walls," she said with a flippancy she really didn't feel.

"Sybil said she had someone coming in, but..." He looked around in disgust. "What did she do—go from door to door searching for whoever would do the worst possible job? Or did you volunteer just to get at me?"

Deanna scrambled off the stepladder and backed away until the desk was between them. "There's nothing wrong with the job I did," she snapped. "It's damned near perfect."

"Perfect! This is the ugliest stuff I've ever seen. Where the hell did you get it—at a reject sale?"

Deanna's chin rose and she glared at him. "Hey, I don't pick the stuff. I just put it up. If you don't like it, why did you buy it?"

"I didn't." He threw up his hands in exasperation. "This is nothing like what I picked out. Surely you must have known there was something wrong. Or did you change it on me?" he asked suddenly, his eyes narrowing again.

"Get real," she muttered. "You're not worth the effort." She took a deep breath and let it out slowly. "I got a phone call yesterday asking me to paper a room. I accepted, then found out it was here. But I thought, hey, I'll do it, anyway. I came this morning and was let in by your friend Sybil, who pointed out the paper and left. I put it up as I was hired to do. That's it. If the store sent the wrong stuff, that's between you and them. It's got nothing to do with me."

"Oh, yes, it does. You put it up, you take it down."

"No way," Deanna said adamantly. "Phone the store. Make them do it. This is not my fault."

He looked around the room again, wincing. "Surely you must have known this was the wrong paper. Why did you go ahead with it?"

Deanna shrugged. "How am I supposed to know what your tastes are? Let me repeat myself. I was told to put this paper up and I did. No hidden motives, no revenge. I did the job I was hired to do, nothing more."

He glanced at his desk with the white mark on the reddish surface. "I suppose the gouge in my desk isn't your fault, either."

She shook her head quickly. "I'm sorry it happened, but the way you came in here yelling like that, you're lucky I didn't fall and hit my head."

"That would really have wrecked the desk," he murmured, then added, "I see you were quick to take the check I left."

Deanna patted the back pocket of her cutoffs. "I did the job. It's mine." But she knew if he put up an argument, she'd return it. It wasn't worth fighting about.

He stared at the paper, rubbing at his brow. "This can't stay up," he said, half to himself. "I'll never get any work done while it's like this. Tell you what—you can keep the check if you get this stuff off the walls. Right away would suit me."

Deanna hesitated. He was being somewhat more reasonable at the moment, and the ridiculous accusations had stopped, but she really didn't owe him anything, and she was overdue for lunch and a cold drink. Still…it might help stop this silly feud that seemed to be developing between them.

"All right," she said reluctantly, pushing the hair back from her face. "But I'm not washing the walls afterward. You can do that."

He raised his well-defined eyebrows as though he was coolly amused at her suggestion. "Will it take you long?" he asked.

"Not nearly as long as it took to put it up. If you leave now, I'll get started."

"Maybe I'll stay and make sure you do a proper job this time."

Deanna glared at him in exasperation. "I did a proper job the first time. Taking it down is a snap. But I would prefer to do it without an audience—a critical audience at that." She jerked a thumb in the direction of the door. "If you don't mind?"

His mouth twitched with what could almost be considered a smile. "I'll be in the kitchen if you want anything."

She had a sudden surprising urge to see that smile expand. "I won't," she said a touch haughtily, and as he left, she wondered just how much a smile would add to his undeniably handsome face.

She started tugging a corner of the paper and peeled it back from the wall with a sigh. All that work for nothing. But at least she had the check. It could have been worse.

THE ALARM SOUNDED much too early. Groaning tiredly, Deanna switched it off and slid out of bed, wishing she could stay home today and write. She paused for a moment to pet the two black cats sleeping in a tangle at the foot of her bed.

"C'mon Alfie. Up and at 'em, Imp," she said. "How can I make my bed with you two all over it?" The cats yawned and stretched, gave each other a halfhearted swipe of the tongue, then settled down to sleep again.

"Lazybones," she said, then made her way to the kitchen. The old gray tom had heard the alarm and was waiting, as he did most mornings, with his nose at the crack of the back door. Deanna let him out and he sauntered into the bright morning.

"Leave the birds alone, Leo," she said, waiting for his tail to clear the door before closing it.

She opened the curtains on the window over the sink, then pulled the cover off the bird cage. The budgies greeted her with an excited little dance and loud squawks.

"A bit quieter, please," Deanna murmured, raking her fingers through her hair. She put the coffee on to brew, then went to shower.

She took a deep breath as she left the house about an hour later. It was a beautiful morning. The air was still fresh, the sky a deep blue, not yet paled by a haze of heat. From a few blocks over, traffic hummed as it converged on the Osborne Street bridge in its rush downtown.

She shot a quick look next door. The beautifully landscaped yard was empty and, thank goodness, there was no sign of her neighbor. She hoped he wasn't going to make an appearance today. She didn't need another confrontation.

After closing the gate, she began to walk down the street under high, arching elm trees. From their gnarled and knotted branches came the twitter of nesting sparrows. She pulled a leaf from a lilac bush and rolled it between her fingers as she continued on her way, enjoying her walk to the store.

Special Moments was a flower shop in Winnipeg's Osborne Village. Trendy stores and restaurants lined the street on both sides just before it crossed the Assiniboine River and ran past the legislative buildings on its way to downtown Winnipeg.

A great variety of people lived in the district. High rises alternated with smaller apartment buildings and expensive condos. Big old houses from another era abounded, some stylishly renovated, others divided into rooming houses grabbed up by students and others with low income. Here and there were single-family homes. Unlike the suburbs, these streets were alive night and day with an interesting mixture of people.

Deanna let herself into the shop with its sweet mingle of odors. She gazed at the flowers ranging from the ordinary to the exotic. It really was a nice place to work.

"It's me, Pat," she called as she made her way through to the back.

Pat Hahn poked her head out from the storage room. "Good morning, Deanna. Lovely day, isn't it?"

"It sure is," Deanna agreed. "So, is it going to be busy today?"

"I expect it will," Pat said with satisfaction. "The flowers for the Symcko wedding are in. I'll get started on the arrangements as soon as I've sorted through them. You can take care of anyone coming in off the street. Oh, and could you put that sign advertising our summer bouquet on the sidewalk? It attracts the impulse buyer. We sold several yesterday. Then come in here. The coffee has just finished brewing, and I got some Danish pastries from the bakery. They're still warm." She withdrew her head from the beaded curtain doorway.

Smiling, Deanna put down her purse and picked up the sign. Pat was in her mid-forties, plump and graying, with a cheerful, slightly befuddled personality. She was fun to work for and had become a good friend. Pushing the door open with her hip, Deanna carefully placed the sign where it would catch the attention of passersby but not impede their passage. Satisfied, she went to join Pat.

After pouring herself a cup of steaming coffee, Deanna perched on the corner of the workbench that took up the length of one wall. She accepted a Danish and bit into the soft, delicious warmth.

"Mmm," she said around the mouthful. "This is great. Thanks, Pat."

Pat popped the remains of a roll into her mouth and reached for another. "I know I shouldn't," she said with a sigh, "but I have absolutely no resistance. Now, you could eat a dozen and not gain an ounce."

"No, but I'd probably be sick." Deanna took another bite, then licked at the icing clinging to her fingers. "I wouldn't mind gaining a bit of weight, though," she said.

"You could use some," Pat agreed. "But you look pretty good just the way you are. Tall and willowy—"

"Tall and scrawny," Deanna interjected. She was just under five ten and, in spite of a healthy appetite, couldn't put on weight.

Pat shook her head. "Not with your style. You look great."

"Thanks," Deanna murmured, a little embarrassed by the compliments. Only one person had ever made her feel beautiful, and he was long gone from her life, except in fleeting dreams and wistful memory.

"But you do look a little tired," Pat said, after swallowing another mouthful of pastry. "Were you writing again last night?"

Deanna nodded. "I couldn't sleep. I had another run-in with my arrogant and self-satisfied neighbor."

"What did you do this time?" Pat asked, her brown eyes sparkling with curiosity.

"I didn't do anything. Well, not on purpose, anyway, although to hear him go on, you'd think I was involved in a major conspiracy against him."

"So tell me—what happened?"

"Well, the wife of one of his co-workers hired me to paper one of the rooms in his house. She got my name from Cynthia—I did her baby's room, remember?"

Pat nodded. "And?" she prompted.

"I papered his den, just like I was supposed to do. But just my luck, the store had delivered the wrong rolls. It had to be the most hideous design I've ever seen, and that includes the pumpkin pattern I put up in that one kitchen."

"That was ugly," Pat said, remembering the sample Deanna had shown her. "And you say this was worse?"

Deanna rolled her eyes and nodded. "Oh, yeah. Little bubble-blowing purple fishes peeking from behind big purple weeds. Anyway, I'd just finished when he came home."

"What did he do?"

"Hit the ceiling, basically. And of course he accused me of putting up the wrong paper on purpose." She shook her head. "I can't believe that man, Pat. Never a smile or a polite comment, nothing pleasant at all. Some neighbor."

"And him a handsome bachelor," Pat teased. "Too bad. So, did you get paid, anyway?"

"I'd already pocketed the check. He calmed down long enough to say I could keep it if I took the stuff down."

"Did you?"

"Yep—and left behind walls streaked with gooey paste." She grinned. "I hope he spent all night scrubbing it off."

Pat chuckled. "From all you've said, I doubt it."

"So do I." She put down her coffee cup and stretched a little, feeling a slight twinge in her shoulder muscles. She rubbed them absently. "There must be a better way to earn a living."

"There is," Pat said cheerfully as the bells on the shop door tinkled. "Get out there and sell some flowers."

"Yes, ma'am." Deanna saluted as she slid off the workbench. Smiling, she went out to greet the first customer of the day.

CHAPTER TWO

NEARLY TWO WEEKS passed before Deanna saw any further sign of life from her neighbor. She'd assumed he was away, and that suited her just fine.

She was walking home from the flower shop late one afternoon. It was hot, car exhaust tainted the air, and the traffic was loud and annoying. She made for a quieter side street where spreading elm trees arched cool shade over the roadway and the air felt fresher.

A young girl was walking just ahead of her, hands jammed deep in the pockets of her cutoffs as she idly kicked at a rock. She glanced curiously over her shoulder as she sensed someone behind her, then skipped away, turning down Deanna's street.

Deanna walked slowly homeward, her mind slipping into a scene she wanted to write. Her imagination took hold and the pictures were vivid. She quickened her pace, her fingers itching to hold a pen.

As she neared her house, she noticed the girl sitting on her neighbor's front steps, chewing on one end of a licorice whip while weaving the other through her fingers. She glanced up as Deanna passed, watching her for a moment.

Deanna doubted the girl had any business being in her neighbor's yard. She stopped and started to say something, then shook her head and continued on. The girl wasn't doing any harm just sitting there. Chances were she just wanted to rest for a few minutes, and the steps had seemed as good a place as any.

Deanna turned into her own yard. *I'll check later,* she thought, fumbling in her bag for the key to the front door. She entered the house, still cool from being closed up all day, kicked off her sandals and went straight into the kitchen to pick up her pen and jot down the scene that had been running through her mind most of the afternoon.

Some time had passed before she thought of the girl again. *I suppose I should go take a look,* she said to herself, putting down her pen. She might not care much for her neighbor, but that didn't mean she couldn't keep an eye on the place when he wasn't around.

As expected, the girl was gone. Satisfied, Deanna went around to her backyard and began pulling the few weeds that had begun to grow in the flower bed that edged the stone wall. She heard a splash from the pool next door and raised her head, listening closely. There was another splash and a soft, murmuring sound.

It could be him, she thought, or... If it was the girl, she should be warned away from the pool and told to stay out of the yard. Deanna climbed quietly onto the bench and risked a quick look over the wall.

It was the girl. She was walking around the pool, using a long-handled net to scoop out bits of fallen leaves, singing softly to herself.

Deanna decided to confront the girl face-to-face. She had to be made to understand that she shouldn't be there and certainly not playing near the water.

Deanna hoisted herself up and over the stone wall, then dropped lightly onto the deck. It was faster than going around.

The girl hadn't heard her.

"Excuse me," Deanna called.

Startled, the girl nearly lost her balance. She teetered on the edge of the pool for a second, net dripping. Regaining her balance, she stared at Deanna.

She was young, no more than eight or nine, with a thin, pale face. Round, light blue eyes held a hint of defiance in their depths.

Deanna came a little closer. "You know, you shouldn't be here."

"Why not?"

"This isn't your house. And it's dangerous to play around water when you're by yourself."

The girl's lips tightened and she shook ragged, dark brown bangs from her eyes. "I live here," she said. "Besides, I can swim real good."

"Maybe you can. But you still shouldn't be here."

"I told you. I live here."

Deanna crossed her arms and tilted her head to one side, looking down at the defiant little face. "No, you don't."

The girl glared at Deanna. "Do so!"

Deanna hid a smile, amused at the child's stubbornness. She decided to try another approach. "What's your name?"

The girl scowled, then answered reluctantly. "Mickey."

"Mickey what?"

A sound of frustration escaped from the tightly held lips. "Wescott."

"All right, Mickey Wescott—where do you really live?"

"I *told* you already!"

"So you did. Okay, how do I get in touch with your parents?"

There was a flicker in the blue eyes. "I don't got any parents."

Something in the girl's voice told Deanna she was telling the truth. "Who looks after you, Mickey?" she asked gently.

"My uncle. But he's at work."

"What's your uncle's name?"

"Lee."

"And his last name?"

"Um . . . Stratton."

Lee Stratton. She had seen the name on the check her neighbor had given her. So the child was telling the truth. Deanna looked at her sympathetically. "Did you just move here, Mickey?"

"Uh-huh. Yesterday."

"Who's supposed to be looking after you while your uncle is at work?" He wouldn't have left Mickey alone, would he? She was far too young to be on her own for any length of time.

Mickey made a face. "Kyra's supposed to. But her boyfriend came over and he got bored and wanted her to leave and go with him to . . . to the Ex?" She looked questioningly at Deanna, not certain of the term.

Deanna nodded. "The Red River Exhibition," she said. "It's a big fair that comes to Winnipeg every year at this time."

"Yeah, well, he wanted to go and not wait until my uncle got home, so Kyra told me to sit and watch TV and went." Mickey raised both hands, palms up, and shook her head as though she couldn't quite believe it.

Deanna chuckled. "I take it Kyra isn't very old."

"She's older'n me and *I* wouldn't take off and leave some little kid all alone. She's kinda stupid."

"It sounds like it," Deanna agreed, her clear gray eyes dancing with amusement. "How old are you, Mickey?"

"Nine. Well, almost nine," she amended. "In August."

And quite mature, Deanna thought, impressed by the child. But certainly not old enough to be alone. "Maybe you should go call your uncle and let him know Kyra left."

"Um...the door locked when I went outside, and I can't get back in."

"Okay, then we can call him from my house."

"I don't know the number. It's by the phone, but I didn't learn it yet."

"How about the name of the place he works? Do you know that?"

Mickey grinned a little ruefully. "Nope."

"Do you know anybody we can phone?"

"No," she said slowly. "I was staying with my uncle's friends. Then my uncle got back and moved my stuff here."

"What are their names?"

"Rick and Sybil. They got a new baby and a dog. Sybil let me help her with the baby. It was neat."

"Do you know their last name?"

Mickey flopped down onto a lawn chair and frowned in thought, her small, pointed chin resting on her hands. "Nope."

"How about where they live? Do you remember?"

"Outside the city—not far, but I don't think I know how to get there." Her shoulders hunched. "I'm sorry," she mumbled after a moment.

Deanna sat down beside her and touched her arm briefly. "Hey—don't worry about it. We'll wait here for your uncle. I'm sure he won't be long."

Mickey looked at her sideways. "I'm kind of hungry," she said.

"You know, so am I. Tell you what—let's go over to my place for some supper."

Mickey's blue eyes studied her intently, then she nodded. "Okay. Have you got any kids?" she asked, getting to her feet.

"No. But I have three cats and two budgies."

Mickey's face lighted up. "Neat! Let's go see them."

Laughing, Deanna followed her out of the yard, carefully locking the gate behind them.

She knew she was doing the right thing. Her conscience would not allow her to leave the child sitting on the steps or playing by the pool waiting for the uncle to return from work, and she certainly didn't want to bring anyone else into it, not at this point, anyway. At the moment, there wasn't much she could do but take Mickey home with her. Even, she thought grimly, if it means facing *him* again. She didn't like the thought of that at all, although it was he who was in the wrong this time, and much more so than she had ever been.

Mickey went willingly with her, looking curiously around as she entered the house. She grinned as the two kittens came from the living room, tails held high.

"They look like twins," she said.

"They're brothers," Deanna smiled at the girl who was already on her knees to play with the cats. "That one is Alfie," she said, pointing, "and the other one is Imp. Leo is probably at the back door wanting to be let in. Let's go see."

Mickey scrambled up as Deanna went through to the kitchen where the two budgies began to chirp and squawk. The girl ran to the cage and peered inside, crooning to the birds. "What're their names?"

"Whirlybird and Tinkerbell."

Mickey wrinkled her nose and giggled. "That's funny. How come you got so many pets?"

"Well, Leo and the birds belonged to my aunt. This is her house. She moved to Victoria last year and thought they'd be better off staying here. And I found the two kittens last winter. Someone had left them in the lane." She opened the door and the gray tom stalked in, ears flat and tail twitching.

Deanna laughed and shook her head. "Leo's mad because I left him out all day. And if I'd left him in, he'd be mad because he couldn't get outside. He thinks someone should be here to open doors for him all day long."

"What's he doing?" Mickey asked as Leo went to the cupboard beside the fridge and sat with his nose close to the crack.

"His food is in there," Deanna explained. "It's his way of telling me to feed him. You can get it out and put some in the bowl if you want."

Mickey nodded. "Okay," she said. "He's pretty smart." She took out the box and carefully poured some into the cats' dish. "Is that enough?" she asked glancing over her shoulder at Deanna.

"A bit more," Deanna said. "There—that's good."

Mickey laughed as Alfie and Imp pushed their way in. "That's neat—a big gray head between two small black ones." She put the food away, then went to kneel beside the cats, carefully stroking each in turn. "I always wanted a kitten," she said. "But we couldn't have one in the apartment."

"Where did you live?" Deanna asked casually.

"In Edmonton, and before that, Calgary. We lived in Saskatoon for a while, too, but I don't really remember that."

"Those are nice cities," Deanna said. She wanted to hear more but didn't want to inundate the child with questions. "I was thinking of having spaghetti for supper. How does that sound?"

"Good. I like spaghetti. With garlic bread. I can make it, if you want."

"Do you promise to use lots of garlic?"

Mickey nodded. "Yep."

"Okay, then, you can make it. Now, let's go wash our hands and get started. I'm starving."

MICKEY CAREFULLY TWISTED spaghetti around her fork and started to raise it to her mouth. She stopped and put her fork down, looking at Deanna, her eyes suddenly serious. "I don't know what your name is."

"I'm sorry, Mickey. My name is Deanna Hamilton. You can call me Deanna."

Mickey nodded and picked up her fork again. "Okay."
She took a mouthful of spaghetti, chewed, then swallowed.
"This is really good. You're a good cook."

"Thanks. Your garlic bread is great. What else can you
make?"

Mickey shrugged her thin shoulders. "Lots of things. I
always made supper when my mom was working."

"She must have appreciated that," Deanna said, wondering about the girl's mother.

"Yeah, she did," Mickey said softly, her eyes clouded and
distant. After a moment of silence, she put her fork down.
"I can't eat any more." She sighed, looking very young and
forlorn. "Could I please go outside for a while?"

"Of course," Deanna said gently. "There's a swing in the
apple tree in the backyard—it's a nice shady place to sit on
a hot day. And there's a robin's nest in the lilac bush beside
the wall. If you sit really quiet, you'll probably see the parents feeding the babies. They just hatched last week."

"Okay." Mickey slid to the floor and pushed her chair
under the table. "Thank you very much for supper," she
intoned politely.

"You're welcome," Deanna replied, and watched the girl
quietly leave the room. Then she pushed her own plate away.
Poor kid, she thought, and wondered again how she came
to be in these circumstances.

As Deanna cleared the table and stacked the plates in the
dishwasher, she suddenly realized her neighbor had no way
of knowing where his niece was. She scribbled a note and
hurried over to tape it to his door. At least now he wouldn't
be able to accuse her of hiding the child on him or something else equally irrational.

Back in the kitchen, she filled two dessert bowls with
chocolate ice cream and took them outside.

The yard was large by city standards, the enclosing wall
of water-smoothed granite stones an attractive feature.

Honeysuckle and lilac pressed against it, softening the effect. An apple and two plum trees spread shade over the lawn toward the back. A vegetable garden grew lush and green in neat, orderly rows. Pale pink roses blossomed next to the shelter of the house, their heady scent filling the early-evening air.

Mickey sat on the swing, staring at the ground as she twirled gently, her dark fall of hair hiding her face. There was a general air of neglect about her. Her clothes were old and shabby, her haircut long grown out. Shaggy bangs hung limply over her eyebrows, and she kept tossing her head to keep them out of her eyes. A scabby scrape was healing on one knee and she looked as if she needed a good scrubbing. Deanna knew that kids didn't stay clean for long on hot summer days, but it seemed as though no one really cared about how this girl looked.

Deanna had noticed how impeccably groomed Lee Stratton was, from his neatly styled hair and stylish clothes, down to his highly polished shoes. She assumed he'd want the same for his niece. Mickey's appearance made her wonder just how wanted the little girl was.

"Mickey," Deanna said as she approached, "I've got dessert." She handed the girl one of the bowls, then sat cross-legged on the grass, arranging her skirt over her knees. "I hope you like chocolate."

"It's my favorite! Thanks."

"Mine, too. Especially on hot days like this." She took a spoonful and let it melt in her mouth. "Mmm, that's good."

Mickey grinned suddenly and nodded. "It sure is." She took another bite.

"What does your uncle do?" Deanna asked.

"He makes computers, him and Rick—they work together. Rick and Sybil have this computer they let me use. They've got all these neat games. It was lots of fun. I think Uncle Lee has one, too, but I haven't seen it yet. I hope he lets me use it." Something in her voice said she doubted he would.

"Do you know if it's a big company?"

"I think so. My mom said he made lots of money."

He would have to, Deanna thought. She knew the house next door had been expensive. Even her aunt's much older, smaller house was worth quite a bit, mainly because of the location and the size of the yard.

Mickey finished her ice cream. "Could we go for a walk?"

"I'd like to," Deanna said, setting her empty bowl on the grass beside her. "But I think we should be here when your uncle gets home."

"I suppose. What time is it now?"

"It was almost seven when I came out."

"Could I go watch TV?"

"If you want."

"Good." Mickey jumped off the swing and started for the house, empty bowl in hand.

IT WAS NINE-THIRTY when Deanna flicked the TV off. She'd had more than her fill of sitcom reruns, but Mickey looked as though she could happily spend the rest of the night in front of the screen.

Mickey glanced at her, then down at the kitten cradled in her lap. "Uncle Lee is really late, isn't he?"

"I imagine that's because he thinks you're with the baby-sitter."

"Yeah, he told her he'd be late sometimes and that he'd pay her extra if he was. She said it was okay." Mickey made a face. "Until she wanted to go out with her stupid boy-friend."

"That was pretty irresponsible of her."

Mickey nodded. She hesitated for a moment, scratching under Imp's chin. "Am I being a bother?"

"No, Mickey," Deanna said quickly. "Of course you're not." It was true. The child was bright and talkative, obviously used to the company of adults. Deanna found her quite entertaining. It was only the thought of the uncle eventually showing up that was unnerving. "I've enjoyed having you here."

Mickey flashed her a quick grin. "I like being here." She looked around the living room with its comfortable clutter of furniture and large, leafy plants. "It's nice."

"I like it, too," Deanna said. She remembered how warm and welcoming the house had seemed when her aunt had taken her in after Ryan's death. It was in this house that she had slowly, painfully, begun to live again and to remember Ryan without being overcome with grief.

She looked closely at the girl. "You're tired, aren't you?"

Mickey nodded reluctantly. "I didn't sleep so good last night. I'm not used to being there yet."

Deanna sensed that there had been a lot of changes in the girl's life recently. "Would you like to have a nice cool shower, then go lie down on my bed? We don't know how long your uncle will be, and there's no point in your waiting up if you're tired."

"Don't you mind?" Mickey asked, not yet reassured.

"Not at all," Deanna said, smiling warmly. "It's nice to have company."

"Okay then. I am kinda hot. Hey—maybe we could go in the swimming pool."

"It might be better if we don't," Deanna said, ushering Mickey into the bathroom. All she could think about was the embarrassment of being caught in her midnight swim, climbing the wall, knowing Lee Stratton's intense eyes watched every movement. The picture had the strength to make her cringe all over again. It was good to know she was in the right this time.

Deanna gave Mickey one of her T-shirts to put on after her shower. As she rolled up the sleeves, she smiled at the little girl and said, "There now. That's as good as a nightgown."

She led Mickey into her bedroom. It would be cooler there than in the spare room, which caught the late sun. The third, downstairs bedroom she used as a den.

Deanna's room had recently been redecorated. The colors were soft, the furniture an antique white. It looked light and attractive.

Mickey glanced around with interest. "This is nice," she said as she sat on the edge of the bed. She saw the picture on the night table. "Is that your husband?" she asked.

Deanna glanced at the picture of Ryan and nodded. "He was."

"Are you divorced?" Mickey asked. She pulled her legs up and wiggled down under the sheet.

"No. He died a few years ago. He'd been sick for a long time."

Mickey's eyes had a faraway look. "Like my mom," she said softly.

Deanna sat beside her. "Your mother was sick?"

Mickey nodded, her face pale and sad. "She just died."

"Oh, Mickey—I'm so sorry." What a terrible loss for such a young child!

Mickey's eyes were awash with tears. "We talked about it lots when she was in the hospital, but I still miss her real bad."

"Of course you do," Deanna murmured, reaching for Mickey's hand. She stroked it comfortingly, her heart going out to the sad and lonely little girl. "It's not easy to lose someone you love."

Mickey stared down at their joined hands. "Do you still miss your husband?"

"Not like at first," Deanna said. Except in dreams on lonely nights or when she made plans for a future that no longer included him or...

She sighed softly. "It does get easier, Mickey. I promise." She hesitated, then asked, "What about your father?"

"He stopped living with us when I was four. I haven't seen him for a long time."

"Is your uncle your mother's brother?"

Mickey nodded. "Mom thought he'd be able to take care of me."

Deanna wondered about that. He hadn't even been able to get a reliable baby-sitter for her. "Do you have any other family?"

"Nope. Unless my dad comes back," she added wistfully, then shrugged. "Uncle Lee's okay. It's just...kind of lonely now."

Deanna squeezed her hand in silent sympathy. "It'll take a little time for you to get used to each other and for his house to feel like home. New friends will make things better, too."

"Yeah, I suppose. I don't have any friends here yet."

"Yes, you do."

Mickey frowned and looked up. "Who?"

Deanna grinned. "Me."

Mickey's face brightened. "And Leo and Alfie and Imp," she added.

"Don't forget Whirlybird and Tinkerbell."

Mickey giggled. "Those are silly names."

"They're silly birds," Deanna said. "Now. Why don't you try and get a bit of sleep? It's getting late."

Mickey slid down and laid her head on the pillow. "Uncle Lee should be here by now." The worried note was creeping back into her voice.

"He'll be home soon, I'm sure. Don't worry about it." Deanna smoothed the edge of the sheet over the girl's shoulders. "I like having you here. You can stay as long as you need to." Impulsively she dropped a kiss on Mickey's cheek. "Get some sleep, sweetie," she said softly. "Everything will be okay."

She went slowly down the stairs, hoping she'd spoken the truth. Could her neighbor provide a decent, caring home for the grieving little girl? Mickey needed a special kind of love and understanding at this time in her life. Could her uncle give that to her?

Having met the man, Deanna strongly doubted it. He seemed far too arrogant, too easily given to anger.

She flopped onto the couch with a sigh. She was going to have to face him again, and soon. The prospect was daunting.

Deanna found it impossible to relax. She turned the stereo on to a soft-rock station, then opened a book and tried to read, but it wasn't long before she put the book aside and began to pace about the house. Every time she heard a car, she peeked through the window. So far none had pulled into the drive of the house next door.

She might be in the right this time, but she wasn't looking forward to another meeting with her neighbor. She wished he would come home so she could get it over with.

Moving quietly up the stairs, she looked in on Mickey. The girl was sleeping, one hand curled over her head, a lock of hair woven through her fingers. The two black cats were curled up on the bottom of the bed. A light breeze pushed through the window, fanning the filmy curtains and cooling the room.

Deanna felt an unexpected tug at her heartstrings. She and Ryan had wanted a child, desperately so, but the combination of his illness and treatments had made that impossible. If only this was their child sleeping peacefully in her bed. Her life would feel so much more complete, even without Ryan. Deanna's sigh was soft and filled with regret as she closed the door and went downstairs to resume her pacing.

Where was the uncle? Working? Entertaining? Either way he hadn't given much thought to his niece's well-being. If he'd bothered to try to call home to wish Mickey good-night or ask how her day had been, he would have suspected something was amiss and he'd be home.

The doorbell chimed suddenly, loudly, then pealed again before she could answer. It rang a third time just as she pulled the door open.

Her neighbor stood there, his angry scowl highlighted by the glare of the porch light. His square jaw jutted out aggressively. "Where's Michelle?" he demanded.

Deanna took a step back. "Michelle? You mean Mickey?"

"How many little girls have you got stashed away in there?" he asked, his lips curling in scorn. "What is she doing here, anyway?"

Refusing to let him intimidate her, Deanna scowled at him. "Well, I could have left her sitting outside on the steps until you decided to crawl back home. Or I could have called the police and let them take her to Children's Aid while you tried to explain why she was locked out of the house until this hour of the night. But I happen to like the kid. I thought this was the best way. For her," she added with emphasis. Her look told him plainly that she couldn't care less about him.

Hazel eyes narrowed suspiciously. "What the hell has been going on around here?"

"Calm down and I'll tell you—but come in. You've probably got half the neighborhood peering out their windows by now." She stood aside to let him enter the house.

He brushed passed her, then turned abruptly. "Is she all right?" he demanded.

"Nice of you to ask," Deanna said, unable to stop the sarcasm. "She's fine. She's asleep. Why don't you lower your voice so she can stay that way while we talk?"

He bit back an angry response. "So talk," he said his lips thin.

"In the living room," she said, forcing herself to speak calmly. It would be too easy to get into a shouting match with this man. "Through there," she gestured, and followed him as he strode into the room.

He stood beside the bookcase, his eyes flashing, his chin thrust forward as he glared at her. The sleeves of his rumpled shirt were rolled up, and the top buttons were open under his tie, which was askew. His straight, light brown hair was damp with perspiration. He looked hot and, beneath his anger, tired.

Working or entertaining? Deanna wondered again as she sat on the edge of the couch and straightened her skirt, giving herself time to calm down.

"Please sit," she said coolly. She had a few things to say to him, and like it or not, he was going to hear them.

He hesitated for a moment, then moved to the armchair opposite her. "All right," he said tightly. "Start explaining. What kind of trouble are you brewing this time?"

Deanna's coolness vanished. The arrogance of the man! "This has nothing to do with me."

"No?" he said in obvious disbelief. "Then explain what my niece is doing in your house."

"Give me a chance and I will," she said, glaring at him.

He glanced deliberately at his watch. "I'm waiting."

Only the thought of the child sleeping upstairs kept her from completely losing control. She drew one angry breath, then another, before telling him how she had found Mickey all alone and locked out of the house with no one to turn to.

By the time she'd finished, his eyes were closed and he was rubbing his forehead as though his head ached. He swore softly under his breath and opened his eyes, looking tiredly at her.

"Thank you," he said stiffly. "I overreacted. I was concerned. I'll take her home now." He started to rise.

Deanna held up a hand. "I'm not finished yet," she said firmly.

He sat back, well-defined eyebrows raised in surprise. "What?"

"I'm not finished," Deanna repeated. A fine line slanted down her brow, and she kneaded the palm of her hand nervously. "Your niece was left without adequate supervision—okay, maybe you couldn't have foreseen it. But you should have gone over some ground rules with her."

His scowl returned. Deanna ignored it and went on. "She should have known not to leave the house, but to phone you right away. As it was, she was locked out, not knowing your work number or, for that matter, the name of the company you work for. She had no way of contacting you. And she should never have come with me, a stranger. She was lucky. So were you—you might never have seen her again. Children disappear every day." There. It had been said. Let him glare at her.

"Lecture over?" he asked.

"Yes." The word seethed with the anger she felt at his tone of voice and the arrogant tilt of his head.

"Good. Now where is she?"

Deanna stood up, her lips tight, and inclined her head toward the hallway. "This way."

He followed her up the stairs, then pushed past her as she opened the door to her room. The two black cats opened their eyes, blinking at the light streaming in from the hallway. Leo wove himself through Deanna's legs and yowled plaintively to be let outside.

"What is this—a damned zoo?" he muttered, making his way to the bed. He pulled back the sheet and bent down to scoop his niece into his arms. She murmured in protest and pushed against his shoulder.

"It's Uncle Lee, Michelle," he said. "I'm taking you home." Her eyes opened wide and she stared for a moment, then relaxed with a sigh.

Alfie and Imp leapt off the bed and trotted in front of him, tails held high. Deanna shooed all three animals downstairs, then went to open the front door.

He stepped onto the porch and turned, his green-flecked eyes cool and distant. Mickey's tousled head rolled slackly against his shoulder. She frowned and muttered something in her sleep.

He nodded. "Thank you," he stated flatly, obviously hating to have to say the words, and left.

Deanna glared at his retreating back. "You're welcome," she muttered, then slammed the door and locked it. Shaking her head, she went into the living room and plopped herself on the couch.

What a cold and unyielding man he was! Totally in the wrong, and still he acted as though she had instigated the whole situation! Just the thought of him made her seethe.

But when she thought of Mickey her anger dissipated. Poor kid. What was it going to be like for the child, living under his roof, especially now, when her grief was new and painful? Would he be able to give her the love she needed?

Deanna doubted it. He was a hard man. Unapproachable, not the type to care for a young and vulnerable child.

Leo jumped up and began bumping his head against her hand. Absently Deanna scratched between his ears, wondering how things were going to turn out for Mickey. She was an endearing child, open and forthright. And very sad and lonely, Deanna added, feeling a pang of sympathy.

"I hope he lets her visit us, Leo," she murmured, scratching the cat's grizzled chin. He might not, out of spite if nothing else. Then she decided that he'd probably find it less of a bother to let his niece visit whenever she wanted.

She sighed as she glanced at the clock on the wall. It wasn't that late, but she was tired after a full day and an almost sleepless night. It was time for bed.

The sheets were rumpled from Mickey's presence. Deanna straightened them, then sat on the edge of the mattress. Out of habit, she picked up the picture from the nightstand. Ryan's smiling, open face looked back at her.

Over three years had passed since he'd lost his battle with leukemia, but she still felt as though he was part of her life, as though he shared her dreams and triumphs.

Deanna smiled at the picture as she put it down, wishing she could talk to him. With a tired little sigh, she crawled into bed and reached to turn out the lamp. She draped the sheet over her midsection, leaving her arms and most of her legs uncovered.

Tired as she was, she kept thinking of Mickey and her uncle, her emotions alternating between pity and a renewed surge of anger. Sleep was a long time coming.

CHAPTER THREE

THE DOORBELL RANG early the next morning. Deanna put down her pen and got up to answer it, stretching the stiffness from her muscles.

Mickey stood on the porch holding out Deanna's T-shirt. "I brought this back," she said, handing it to her.

Deanna smiled. "Thanks, Mickey. I still have your things. Can you visit for a moment?"

Mickey shrugged her thin shoulders. "I guess. Uncle Lee didn't say to hurry back. Can I see the cats?" she asked as she came in.

"Sure. They're in the backyard trying to figure out how to get at the robin's nest."

"Can they?" Mickey followed Deanna down the hall and through the kitchen to the back door.

"No. There's no place to climb up to where the nest is. They like to sit close by, though. I just hope they aren't around when the babies start to fly. There—see?" She pointed. The two black cats lay half-hidden under a yellow-flowered potentilla bush. Leo, pretending disdain, crouched beside the apple tree.

Deanna watched as Mickey squatted down to call the cats. The kittens came out like twin shadows and bumped against her outstretched hand. After a moment, Leo strolled over haughtily, tail twitching.

Mickey petted each in turn. "Leave those babies alone, guys," she admonished. "Eat cat food."

Deanna dropped down on the grass. "What did you do today?" she asked.

Mickey sat cross-legged, holding Alfie in her arms while Imp brushed against her. "Uncle Lee took me to work with him," she said. "It was kinda boring, except when he let me play some computer games. And—" her eyes sparkled "—when he phoned Kyra to bawl her out for leaving me alone. That was neat. He even talked to her mom. Bet she got it."

"Did he talk to you, too, Mickey?"

Mickey rolled her eyes and nodded. "Yeah—the big lecture. Now I know the phone number and the place where he works—and not to go with strangers." She grinned at Deanna. "Are you a weirdo?"

Deanna grinned back. "What do you think?"

"Nah. But Uncle Lee said I should have been more careful, that with all those cats and that wild hair, you could have been a witch or something, and I'm lucky you didn't bake me in your oven or steal me away on your broom. Just kidding." She giggled. "I told him you're too pretty to be a witch."

"Thanks, kid," Deanna said dryly, wondering what her neighbor's response to that remark had been. She wasn't going to ask. She patted her untamable shoulder-length hair. It was very curly, a shade caught somewhere between red and light brown, cut to make the unruliness seem intentional. "So, are you getting another baby-sitter?"

"I guess, if Uncle Lee can find one." Mickey put down the cat she was holding and picked up the other. "I wish I didn't have to have a baby-sitter." She glanced sideways at Deanna, "It would be nice if I could just come over here, instead, and have you look after me."

"Your uncle will have other ideas, I'm sure," Deanna said carefully. "But you know you can come and visit anytime you like. As long as you check with him first. And try not to worry, Mickey. I'm sure he'll find someone nice to look after you this time."

Mickey stared at her wistfully, her disappointment obvious. "I s'pose. I don't like to be a bother to him."

"I don't expect you are," Deanna said, wondering if she was speaking the truth. Right now Mickey really needed to feel as though she belonged, not a burden. "It's going to take a bit of time for the two of you to get used to living with each other. It's only been a few days, after all."

Mickey rubbed her chin over the cat's head, her eyes troubled. "I guess. Still . . . I wish nothing changed. I wish my mom didn't have to die."

"I know, sweetie," Deanna said gently, feeling tears sting her eyes. "I know." She put a hand on Mickey's thin little shoulder and gave it a comforting squeeze. Poor child.

She sat silently for a moment, then said, "I was thinking of walking to the corner for an ice-cream cone. Why don't we go ask your uncle if you can come with me?"

Mickey brightened. "Okay!" She put the cat down and scrambled to her feet. "C'mon, Deanna. Let's go."

Deanna followed her, her brow burrowed in thought. She empathized with Mickey, knowing the grief and loneliness she must be feeling, and wanted to help her. The girl needed love and understanding, and Deanna was certain she wasn't getting them from her uncle.

Deanna waited outside while Mickey went in to ask permission. She was back in a few moments, Lee right behind.

He leaned against the door frame, arms crossed over his chest. "You want to take Michelle for ice cream."

The insolent glint in his hazel eyes angered her. "Is it allowed?" she asked with a haughty tilt to her head.

He straightened and glanced at his watch. "Have her back in half an hour." Turning abruptly, he went into the house, shutting the door behind him.

Deanna stared at the closed door in amazement.

"Uncle Lee's kind of tired," Mickey said in a worried voice. Her pale blue eyes were wide with concern as she looked at Deanna. "He's working real hard right now, he told me. He's doing something important, and it has to be finished soon."

"He does seem rather tired," Deanna said evenly, trying to mask her anger. She smiled at Mickey. "So, should we go get that ice cream?"

Mickey gave a little skip and flashed her irrepressible grin. "Okay!"

DEANNA POPPED the last bit of cone into her mouth as they approached Mickey's house. "I'd like to talk to your uncle for a minute," she said, wiping her hands on a paper napkin.

Mickey chased a melting drop of ice cream with her tongue, then glanced up at Deanna. "Did I do something wrong?"

Deanna tweaked a lock of the girl's hair. "Of course not. I just want to ask him something."

Mickey ran for the front door and held it open for Deanna. "I'll go get him."

Deanna shut the door behind her and waited, looking about. The open space with its clean, modern lines and pale, rather sparse decor would have seemed cool even without the aid of central air-conditioning.

Mickey came down a wide hall that was flooded with natural light. Her uncle followed slowly. He had showered and changed while they were gone, and looked more relaxed. But his frown was sharply evident as he came closer.

Deanna turned to Mickey and smiled. "You've got a smudge of chocolate on your face, kiddo," she said.

Mickey gave her mouth a swipe with the back of her hand.

"Missed it," Deanna said lightly. "Better use a mirror."

Mickey looked up at her shrewdly, then nodded. "Okay. I'll be right back." She started down the hallway.

Lee Stratton stood with his hands in his pockets, well-defined brows rising sharply over green-flecked hazel eyes. "What do you want?"

"Mickey's worried about having to get used to another baby-sitter," Deanna said in her straightforward style. "She's had to cope with a lot of changes in her life lately. Maybe you should consider taking some time off, or bringing her to work with you for a while—give her a chance to adjust."

Lee's frown deepened and his lips thinned in anger. "What I do with my niece is no one's concern but my own."

"Someone's got to tell you what she's feeling! She obviously won't tell you herself. I'm not interfering, I just—"

"You're interfering," he cut in, eyes flashing.

Deanna scowled in pure frustration. All she wanted to do was help Mickey. She tried another tactic. "Did you find a baby-sitter?" she asked.

A mocking smile curled his lips and he nodded knowingly. "I was wondering when this would come up."

"What?" Deanna asked, puzzled.

He made a low sound of derision. "Michelle's been carefully dropping your name all day long, letting me know how much she'd like to have you look after her. You obviously put her up to it, although why a woman your age would want to spend the summer baby-sitting is beyond me."

Eyes wide with indignation, she started to speak, sputtered, then tried again. "This is crazy," she muttered angrily. "You're crazy!"

He shrugged. "I must be. I'm actually considering it. You certainly couldn't be any worse than that teenage bimbo I hired. And I must admit, it would be convenient, since you live right next door."

Speechless, Deanna stared at him. He was serious. Even with all he had against her, he would still think about putting her in charge of Mickey for the summer.

"Would you?" he asked bluntly.

"No."

"Why not? I got the impression you don't work. I could make it worth your while."

"I do work," she said with a toss of her head. "Part-time, at a florist. And I do wallpapering on the side."

"I remember," he said dryly. "So, you won't consider taking care of Michelle until school starts?"

The nerve of this man! Deanna started to tell him just what he could do with his arrogant attitude and his job offer when she saw Mickey coming slowly down the hall, looking anxiously from one adult to another.

Deanna's anger disappeared, replaced by concern. If Lee would contemplate hiring her, someone he neither trusted nor liked, who would he eventually bring in to care for Mickey?

Lee read her sudden indecision. "Well?" he asked.

Deanna let out a sharp breath of frustration. "Maybe we'd better talk about this later."

He glanced at his watch. "About nine-thirty?"

She glared at him. "Okay," she muttered, then turned to smile at Mickey.

Mickey came up to her. "Are you leaving, Deanna?"

"Yes." Deanna touched her shoulder lightly. "It's time for me to get back to the cats. Maybe I'll see you tomorrow."

"Prob'ly. I'll come outside with you."

Deanna offered a polite goodbye for Mickey's sake. "Good night, Mr. Stratton," she said coolly.

"Good night," he returned. "Oh, and one more thing... Bring references.

Deanna's eyes flashed with anger, but before she could say anything, he'd walked away.

"Did I give you enough time?" Mickey asked anxiously. "I kinda figured you wanted me to go so you could talk to Uncle Lee alone."

"I did have a couple of things to say to him. Thanks, Mickey. And don't worry. You didn't do anything wrong."

"Good. I tried to think about what I'd done, but..." She shrugged. "I couldn't think of anything bad. Not today, anyway," she added with a sigh.

Deanna laughed and tweaked a scraggly lock of the girl's hair. "That's a relief. Well, good night, Mickey. See you tomorrow."

Mickey smiled her sweet, trusting smile and Deanna's heart gave a queer little flip. She was such an endearing child . . . and so very needy.

"Good night, Deanna," Mickey echoed, and added happily, "See you tomorrow."

Deanna let herself back into the house, feeling a low burn of anger when she thought of Lee Stratton. She dropped her key on the table under the hall mirror and went into the kitchen.

Pouring herself a glass of iced tea, she took a sip, then set it down on the counter and paced restlessly about the room. She had come close to exploding, telling that man exactly what she thought of him. If Mickey hadn't appeared when she had . . . Deanna still seethed.

He thought her childish and vengeful, yet was still willing to hire her to look after Mickey. If she turned him down, who would he bring in? His first choice had proven a disaster. His next could be even worse, and it would be Mickey who suffered.

She couldn't deny the bond that had grown so quickly between her and the girl. She knew Mickey felt it, too.

No, her doubts about taking on the job centered solely around her neighbor. He was cold and arrogant and accusatory—and made her crazy with anger. But what about Mickey, who needed love and caring to help her learn to live with the loss of her mother?

Instinct told Deanna that she could make a difference in Mickey's life, and her sense of rightness demanded that she try.

And it needn't be one-sided. *She* would benefit, as well. It would be good to spend time with someone Mickey's age—the girl was just a little bit younger than the children her books were aimed at. Mickey could give her some real insight into what kids wanted to read. And the girl was delightful company. Deanna was sure they could have fun together.

Mickey would like it. She needed someone she could talk to about the grief dominating her young life. She certainly couldn't turn to her uncle, a man obviously willing to do his duty but not wanting to be inconvenienced further. Mickey was a bright and perceptive girl. She would know exactly how he felt.

Deanna made up her mind. She glanced at the time, then made a phone call to Pat Hahn.

As it turned out, Pat was glad to accommodate. "Your not working for me, Deanna, will give me excuse to roust Kendra, that lazy teenage daughter of mine, out of bed in the mornings," she said. "It'll do her good to work a bit this summer, instead of wandering around with her hand out for spending money and mooning over pimply-faced boys."

Deanna laughed. "Go easy on the kid, Pat. Try to remember what it was like."

"I'm trying." Pat sighed. "I'm trying. But it's been a long time since I was sixteen. So, you're sure about this babysitting thing? I mean, with *him?*"

"I can handle Lee Stratton," Deanna said, then added, "I think. But I want to do this for Mickey. She's a great kid, Pat, and she needs someone right now. It'll be good for both of us. Now, if only he doesn't change his mind just to be contrary."

"He's nuts if he does," Pat said. "Anyway, come in tomorrow and fill me in on the details. You know how I like details."

"You mean gossip."

"Whatever. See you tomorrow."

"See you." Smiling, Deanna replaced the receiver, then went to the fridge for another ice cube for her drink. She leaned against the counter, sipping slowly, wondering if he would change his mind. Who could tell? He had started off by accusing her of putting Mickey up to the whole idea, then abruptly switched to a serious, so it seemed, offer.

Deanna knew one thing for sure. She wasn't going to take any more of his rudeness. Surely to heaven he could deal with her in a reasonably polite manner!

IT WAS OBVIOUS to Deanna as soon as Lee Stratton answered the door that he had decided to hold a proper interview. That was fine with her. At least she'd have an idea of what to expect, and tempers wouldn't flare—she hoped. She relaxed a little as he showed her into his den.

She glanced around the room. It looked much like it had the first time she'd seen it, except for the untidy stacks of computer printouts cluttering the desk. The streaks of paste that had dulled the walls after she had taken down that hideous paper had been washed off.

She took the chair in front of the desk and smoothed her skirt over her knees. "Nice walls," she said demurely.

Startled, Lee stared at her, then a slow smile lightened his face.

It was a very attractive smile, and something told her it wasn't as rare as she'd first thought. She also knew she wanted to see it again. She looked away quickly.

"They are, aren't they?" he said dryly, taking his seat behind the desk. He picked up a pen and tapped it absently on the computer keyboard.

"Do you think there's even a remote possibility we can conduct this interview peacefully?" he asked. Laughter hid in his voice.

The unexpected humor took Deanna by surprise. "That's entirely up to you," she said primly, then answered his smile, unable to resist its appeal.

He sat back in his chair and studied her through half-closed eyes. "This has not been as one-sided as you seem to think."

Was there another meaning to his words, or was it just her imagination? Imagination, Deanna told herself firmly, ignoring the flutter in her stomach.

"Well, I think it has," she said, then added quickly, "Now, about Mickey...."

"Yes, of course." He straightened, leaning his elbows on the gleaming desktop. "Are you interested in looking after her for the rest of the summer?"

"I might be," she said carefully, not wanting him to know how quickly she had taken to the idea.

"All right then. I'd like to know *why* you would consider it."

The question was reasonable and asked in a nice enough manner. "Well, for one, I'm a writer," Deanna answered. "Of children's books—preteens, actually, about Mickey's age. I realize I don't have much contact with children—at least, not on a day-to-day basis. This would be a good chance. But more than that, I like Mickey. I'd enjoy spending time with her."

There was a defiant tilt to her head as she spoke. She'd expected him to break in with some disparaging remark, but he said nothing, merely nodding once or twice. She reached into her skirt pocket and pulled out a folded piece of paper.

"Here are the references you wanted," she said, tossing it onto the desk.

Lee took the paper and unfolded it, glancing quickly at the names. "Okay. So, tell me about yourself."

Deanna raised her hands and looked at him questioningly. "What do you want to know?"

"Everything—more than I got from the last one. I made one mistake. I'm not about to make another."

Deanna could tell from the look on his face that mistakes were something this man rarely made, something he simply didn't tolerate. She felt a pang of sympathy for Mickey.

"Well," she began, "I'm twenty-eight. I've lived next door for the past three years—I rent from my aunt, who is now living in Victoria, B.C. Until last year I worked for an advertising firm—the name is on that list I gave you. Right now I'm working part-time in a flower shop—also on the list—and taking on odd jobs to support myself while I write."

"So this will be just another odd job to you."

"No, not really. As I said, I like Mickey. She and I could have an enjoyable summer, and...I feel Mickey needs more than a baby-sitter. She needs a confidante...a friend. I think I could be that for her."

Lee leaned forward, looking at her sharply. "She's talked to you about her mother?"

"A little. And she also told me that no one knows where her father is."

Lee's lips tightened grimly. "Just as well. She's better off without him, and so would my sister have been, but she'd never listen to—" He stopped abruptly and shook his head. "You're right," he said, returning to the original subject.

"Mickey needs more than a baby-sitter. I'm too busy with work to give her much time.

Deanna had a feeling that was probably fine by him. She couldn't resist asking, "What do you do?"

"I'm a partner in Winntech Computer Graphics," he answered.

"I've heard of it," Deanna said, thinking back to a newspaper article she'd read. It was one of Winnipeg's most successful companies, their initial profits made from sales of some rather remarkable designs for computer games. More recently, they'd turned to designing software to aid architects, graphic artists and animators. The company was built around the sale of ideas rather than manufactured goods. Deanna imagined it must be a very demanding business.

"I work long hours," he said. "I won't be coming home at five every night. Are you prepared for that? And the occasional weekend? I travel."

"I'm sure I can handle it. If I really need to go out, I can arrange for someone else to be with her."

"What do you expect to be paid?"

"What are you offering?" she countered.

Her eyes widened at the figure he mentioned. "That includes evenings—you'll be paid extra when I go out of town," he said. "And I want you to take her shopping for clothes. She hardly has anything decent. I'll give you money for that. You can get groceries, too. Maybe you can get a proper meal down her once in a while—she's a picky eater. And she could use some toys and books—whatever you think she needs." His tone was abrupt, his words to the point. Once again, he was all business and issuing orders.

He glanced back at Deanna's references. "I'll be phoning these people tomorrow, and if they check out, you've got the job." He folded the paper and placed it in his shirt pocket. "I'll let you know tomorrow night," he said, standing up. "I can take Michelle to the office again. One more day won't hurt."

You or the child? Deanna wondered, getting up quickly. "I can see myself out," she said politely.

He nodded. "Right, then. I'll talk to you late tomorrow."

Deanna stopped in the doorway and turned, her gray eyes sparkling. "Oh, I forgot—I promise not to let Mickey anywhere near my oven," she said, unable to resist. "And I won't take her up on my broom no matter how much she wants a ride." Solemnly she touched two fingers to her chin. "Witch's honor."

She slipped through the door before he could say anything, chuckling at the look of surprise on his face. Walking quickly through the house, she let herself out the front door.

Even after her last remarks, she felt confident she would get the job. He would go through the motions of checking her references, but she was pretty sure he had already made up his mind. He really did want more than a baby-sitter for Mickey. He wanted someone to take over his responsibilities, and he was willing to pay well. Lee Stratton might have taken his niece into his home, but she didn't have a place in his heart.

PAT WRAPPED a bouquet of summer flowers and labeled them for delivery. "I got a phone call about you this morning," she said, looking over the top of her glasses at Deanna.

"I expected you would. Did you tell him how wonderful I am?"

"I shoveled it on," Pat said, grinning. "So, is he as sexy as he sounds?"

Deanna looked thoughtful as she rolled a fading rose petal between her fingers. "He is attractive," she admitted finally, as much to herself as to Pat.

"Details, Deanna," Pat urged. "Is he short, tall, fat, thin? C'mon."

Deanna laughed. "Okay, let's see. He's not much taller than I am—"

"Who is?" Pat interrupted.

Deanna looked at her with a sigh of exasperation. "Do you want the details or not?"

"Go on, go on. He's fairly tall," she prompted.

"A nice build, not muscle-bound, but very erect...lithe," she said, remembering the play of light and shadow on his body as he'd stood on the edge of the pool. "His hair is brown, kind of streaky from the sun and styled perfectly. And his eyes are hazel, but more green than brown. His face is, well, very handsome, actually. Strong, but intellectual-looking."

Pat chortled, her brown eyes sparkling. "Oh, yeah? Do I sense an attraction behind all those words?"

Deanna shook her head quickly, a little embarrassed. She hadn't realized just how much she had noticed about Lee Stratton until she spoke. He was attractive, but...

"You have to like someone to be attracted to him," she said firmly. "He might look handsome, but he's far from nice. He's rude and arrogant. Insensitive. And it's pretty obvious he took Mickey into his home only because she had no where else to go, not because he cares about her. She's an obligation—and she knows it."

"It takes time, Deanna. Love doesn't come on order."

"But she's such a great kid. It would be hard *not* to love her. I've got a feeling he lives for his job and not a lot else."

"If he's as good-looking as you say, there's bound to be a girlfriend or two stashed away somewhere. Maybe he'll get married and they'll all live happily ever after. Don't worry about it so much."

Deanna sighed. "I suppose I shouldn't. Well," she added, brightening, "I may not be able to give Mickey a happy home, but I can give her an interesting summer. It should be fun."

Pat was watching her thoughtfully. "I've got a feeling it's going to be."

Deanna caught her tone. "What do you mean by that?"

"Oh, I can't help wondering about this neighbor of yours. There's something in your voice when you talk about him, Deanna. I think I smell romance."

Deanna stared at her as if she was totally crazy. "Those are flowers you smell, Pat, not romance. I've had all that, and it's not going to happen again. And certainly not with him!"

Pat nodded in sympathetic agreement. But she didn't look convinced.

MICKEY STOOD ON THE PORCH, hopping excitedly from one foot to the other. Lee stood back a bit, his lips curling with just a hint of cynicism.

"Uncle Lee says you're gonna look after me," Mickey said, gazing up at Deanna. Her thin little face was split by a huge grin. "That's neat."

Deanna smiled at the girl. "I think so, too. We should have a pretty good summer, right, kid?"

"Yep. For sure. Can I go see the cats?"

"Of course. And you could change the birds' water if you want. I was just going to do it."

"Okay." Mickey scampered past Deanna and skipped down the hallway.

Deanna turned to Lee. "Would you like to come in?"

"No, this is fine." He studied her with distant eyes. "I made those phone calls today," he said. "It seems unanimous—you're a paragon of virtue and industry."

Deanna ignored the edge of sarcasm in his voice. For Mickey's sake she was determined to keep things as calm as possible. Friendly would have been nice, but that seemed out of the question.

"Thank you." She sat on the porch railing, swinging one sandal-clad foot gently back and forth. "Do I start tomorrow?"

He nodded leaning against a post, his arms folded. "I'll bring her here when I leave for work. About eight-thirty?"

"That's fine."

He straightened and dug into his pocket. "Here," he said, handing her a key. "This is for the front door—feel free to come and go as you please. I don't expect you to remain here. I'm sure you'll be wanting to use the pool." Humor, once again completely unexpected, colored his voice.

She took the key from him, surprised at the teasing glint she caught in his eyes as they swept lazily over her.

Without warning, a little spark of awareness pinged through her. She blinked and looked away. "I'm sure we will," she murmured. She glanced at him, but the glint was gone and he was all business again.

He took his wallet from his back pocket. "Like I said yesterday, Michelle needs clothes and things. Take her shopping and get her what she needs." He handed her some money.

Deanna folded the bills and held them in her hand, feeling a little uncomfortable. Still, it would be fun to take Mickey shopping, and it was obvious the girl needed new clothes. Everything she had seen her in looked shabby and too small.

"What time do you expect to be home most nights?" she asked.

He shrugged. "It's hard to say. Right now, I'm negotiating a deal with a California company. I prefer to stay until they close down for the day, which is seven our time. Oh, that reminds me—it's likely I'll be going out that way sometime next week. The details haven't been worked out yet, but I'll probably be gone for two or three days. Is there any problem with Michelle staying with you? I'll pay extra, of course."

"It's no problem. I don't have any plans and I'll enjoy her company." And the extra money would be nice, she thought. With any luck, she could replenish her savings. By the time Mickey went back to school, she wouldn't have to take day jobs to support her writing habit—at least for a while. In the meantime, she would just have to try to write whenever she could.

Lee glanced toward the doorway. "If you have no more questions, I'll take her home now."

"I'll send her over in a few minutes," Deanna said. "If that's all right with you."

He shrugged lazily. "Whatever suits you. I'll see you in the morning."

Deanna made a little face at his retreating back before going into the house and dropping the key and wad of money on the hall table. She could hear Mickey in the kitchen cooing to the birds and went to join her.

"Did you get the water changed okay?" she asked.

"Yep. Whirlybird's afraid of me, but Tinkerbell's not. She sat on my finger. She *is* a she, isn't she?" Mickey asked, looking up at Deanna through her shaggy fall of hair.

Deanna laughed and brushed the hair back from the girl's forehead. "They both are. So, I take it you like the idea of me looking after you this summer."

Mickey nodded decisively. "I was worried he'd find someone else like Kyra, or that I'd have to go with him all the time to his work. That's really kinda boring. Did he go home?"

"Yes. You can stay for a few minutes yet, though. Would you like some lemonade?"

"Yes, please." Mickey climbed onto a wicker stool and sat swinging her legs back and forth. "What are we going to do tomorrow?"

Deanna poured lemonade into glasses filled with ice cubes and handed one to Mickey. "Your uncle would like me to take you shopping. Maybe we should start by going through your things and deciding what you need. And maybe we could find time to get you a haircut."

Mickey grinned and shook her head so that her hair whipped against her face. "Good idea." Her animation disappeared suddenly, and she poked at the ice cubes floating in her drink, her eyes glazed and distant. "My mom always used to cut my hair," she said in a quiet voice.

"She must have done a good job," Deanna said softly, feeling a rush of sympathy.

Mickey nodded and sighed, her shoulders slumping. "I guess I don't really want this," she said, holding out her glass.

Deanna took it from her and set it on the counter. "Would a hug help?"

Mickey looked at her and said nothing, but Deanna sensed she wouldn't object. She went to the girl and gathered her into her arms. Mickey was stiff for a moment, then exhaled sharply and relaxed. Her arms crept up around Deanna's neck, and she snuggled against her shoulder.

Deanna laid her cheek against the top of Mickey's head, her eyes filling with tears. Poor baby, she thought. She was so alone.

"I haven't had a hug for a long time," Mickey said, her voice muffled.

"Neither have I," Deanna said. "It feels good, doesn't it?" Somehow it didn't surprise her that Lee Stratton hadn't hugged his niece. She hadn't sensed any real affection between the two of them. He had taken Mickey in out of a sense of duty and nothing more.

Deanna's lips tightened in frustration, and she hoped that time would forge some kind of bond between the two of them. Mickey needed love, and if Lee couldn't provide it, then maybe he should look for someone who could. She gave the girl another squeeze before releasing her. "Then it's settled. We'll get in some serious shopping tomorrow. Let's start early, okay?"

"Okay," Mickey said. She reached for her glass and took a sip. "Can we eat lunch out?"

"Sure can."

"McDonald's?"

"Where else?"

"Mmm, great! Maybe I'll go home now and have a bath and get ready for tomorrow." She looked up at Deanna as they walked down the hall to the door. "If you go to sleep early, it comes faster you know."

"I remember," Deanna said, and smiled. "See you in the morning, sweetie." She dropped a light kiss on the top of her head.

"Night," Mickey said, then skipped up the sidewalk and into the next yard.

Deanna stayed in the open doorway watching two young children race their tricycles down the opposite sidewalk. She wondered about Mickey's mother, thinking she couldn't have been much like Lee. To have raised such a loving and caring daughter, she must have been open and affectionate.

He was an attractive man all right, but he wasn't a caring man. Was he as cool and distant in his relationships with women—or did he even take the time from running his business to have relationships? Deanna hoped so. She hoped there was a woman in his life, someone who would soften him, help him make a happy home for Mickey.

Sighing, Deanna went inside to write. It took her a while to clear her mind, but soon the words began to flow and she was absorbed in imaginary and faraway worlds, full of rainbow skies and magic.

CHAPTER FOUR

THE SOUND OF THE DOORBELL penetrated her sleep, and in her dream she got up and tried to answer. Another insistent chime woke her, and she blinked in confusion around the sunlit room. A glance at the clock radio on the night table told her it was almost eight-thirty, and she leapt out of bed with a groan of dismay as the doorbell pealed again.

Pulling on a short robe, she tied the sash on her way down the stairs. She paused to grimace at her reflection in the hall mirror and made a futile attempt to tame her hair. Chastising herself for oversleeping, she straightened the collar of her robe, then opened the door.

Lee and Mickey stood on the porch. Deanna gave Mickey a sleepy smile, then turned to Lee.

"I'm sorry," she said hastily. "I worked late last night. I should have set the alarm."

Green-flecked eyes took in her disarray, lingering on the long expanse of her legs, milky white with a nutmeg dusting of freckles. Deanna shifted uneasily, tightening her arms across her chest and wishing she'd had time to shower and dress. There was something too intimate about the way he was studying her.

Lee himself was impeccably groomed, every hair in place. His pale gray suit fitted him perfectly, enhancing his litheness while giving him a businesslike air of competency. Damn, but he was a good-looking man, she thought.

Their eyes met for a brief moment, and Deanna saw a flash of something other than the criticism she expected.

Something warm and approving, like a compliment unspoken. She looked quickly away, made uncomfortable by the little trickle of response she felt deep inside.

She pushed at her hair and turned her attention to Mickey.

"I see you're all ready to start the day."

Mickey nodded. "I had breakfast and everything."

"Good. Well, come on in." She stood aside and let the child enter, then smiled politely at Lee. "We'll see you sometime this evening then." The sooner he left, the better, she thought uneasily. He didn't exactly stare, but he watched too closely, an unexpected interest flickering in that cool gaze.

He nodded curtly. "I'll phone this afternoon and give you a more definite time. If you're not home, I'll leave a message on the machine."

"I don't have an answering machine," Deanna said.

"Then I'll leave it on mine. You can check later." He glanced at his watch. "I've got to go. I'll see you tonight, Michelle." He gave his niece a slight smile, then strode away.

Breathing an audible sigh of relief, Deanna closed the door. "I need coffee," she said. "Let's go into the kitchen."

She pulled the cover off the bird cage and smiled at Mickey's expression as the two birds chirped and danced sideways along the perch, excited by the new day. While the coffee brewed, she cleared her papers from the table.

Mickey watched curiously.

"What's that?" she asked.

"It's a book I'm writing." Deanna stacked the papers on top of the fridge. "It's about a young girl who lives in the future, in space."

Mickey sat down at the table and propped her chin on her hands. "Is it for kids?"

"Yes. For girls a bit older than you." She glanced at the coffeemaker and wished it would hurry. She hadn't had nearly enough sleep. The caffeine would be welcome. "There's one already published. Maybe you could read it sometime."

Mickey made a face. "I don't like reading very much. It's boring."

"Oh? That's too bad." Deanna poured herself a cup of coffee and added milk. She took a sip and sighed. It tasted great. "I was thinking wc could rcad together this summer, out in the backyard. That was one of my favorite things to do when I was a girl."

"Did you read with your mom?"

Deanna shook her head. Neither of her parents had had time or inclination for shared moments like that. "By myself," she said. "But I thought it would be fun if you and I took turns reading aloud. Maybe we could try it sometime. Who knows? You might enjoy it." That was one goal for the summer, she thought determinedly.

Mickey raised her thin shoulders in a shrug. "Are Alfie and Imp here?" she asked, changing the subject.

"In the backyard. Why don't you run out and play with them while I take a shower?"

"Okay." Mickey slid off the chair and went to the door.

"Stay in the yard, okay? I won't be long." She stood leaning against the counter, watching Mickey call the cats. She swallowed the rest of her coffee, then, yawning and stretching, went to shower and dress.

DEANNA KICKED OFF her sandals and sat cross-legged on the floor in Mickey's room. She shook out several brightly colored T-shirts and removed the tags before handing them to Mickey.

Mickey had obviously enjoyed their day of shopping. Her eyes were shining and her expression was bright. The new haircut helped. Glossy bangs feathered across her forehead and tapered down the sides of her thin face to a short blunt cut that curled under just below her ears. It suited her and would be easy to care for.

Within a few minutes, all the new clothes had been put away.

"You bought me a lot of things," Mickey said.

"Your uncle did," Deanna corrected. "I just helped you pick out what you needed. Remember to thank him when he comes home. Now, let's order some pizza. I'm starving."

While they waited for the delivery, they unrolled Mickey's new posters and tried to decide where to put them. Three were of kittens, one was a unicorn.

"The unicorn can go over the bed," Mickey said. "And the kittens on the wall by the window. The three white ones sleeping in a basket can go in the middle."

"That should look good. Where are those thumbtacks we bought?"

"Um, here." Mickey handed her a small bag.

With Mickey standing back and giving her directions, Deanna tacked the posters to the wall.

"There," she said when the last one was up. "How does it look?"

"Lots better," Mickey said. "It's more friendly in here now."

"Didn't you bring any of your own things with you?" Deanna asked. The room had been as sterile and impersonal as the rest of the house, with no jumble of stuffed animals on the bed, no dolls, no shelves of books and games.

"Just my clothes and things. I forgot some stuff at the foster lady's house when Uncle Lee came and got me. I don't know where the rest is. I don't know what happened to my mom's things." She slouched down on the bed, kicking her feet back and forth. "It was all still in the apartment when she had to go to the hospital. I guess someone else has it now."

Surely Lee must have gone through his sister's belongings and brought back something—pictures, if nothing else. He should have seen to it that Mickey had something to remind her of her mother. How could he be so insensitive? Deanna wondered angrily. Once again she felt fiercely glad she had decided to look after Mickey for the summer. The poor kid needed someone who cared.

Mickey pulled the little clock radio they had bought from its box and placed it carefully on the dresser. She plugged it in and found a rock station, grinning at Deanna as she turned up the volume.

"Now it won't be so quiet around here," she said.

Good, Deanna thought, again admiring Mickey's spunk. At least there was now one room in the house where Mickey could feel at home.

"Okay," she said. "Let's get these bags picked up and put in the garbage. Here's a big one—stuff the others in it. And make sure there aren't any pins lying around. You wouldn't want to step on one in your bare feet."

Before they could get started, the doorbell rang. Mickey's head shot up. "Pizza!"

Laughing, Deanna handed her some money. "Better hurry before it gets cold."

I suppose we can eat in here, she thought as Mickey scampered out of the room. The dining area off the kitchen with its glass-top table and modern chairs wasn't the place for gooey pizza in a greasy cardboard box. The kitchen, with its sterile white walls and gleaming, touch-me-not appliances, wasn't much more inviting.

The whole house called out for color and texture, anything that would add warmth and life. Her home would never win any awards for decor, but at least it was comfortable and welcoming, with an atmosphere that said someone lived in it. She wondered if Lee preferred the stark look, or if he simply didn't have the inclination to add his own personal touches. She grinned to herself. Maybe the sight of little purple fishes swimming around his den had been enough to make Lee think twice about decorating.

Mickey came back into the room carefully carrying the pizza box with a brown bag balanced on top. "Here it is," she said and put it down on the dresser. "Mmm. Smells great."

"Then let's eat."

They sat cross-legged on the carpet with the pizza between them, using a bath towel as a picnic blanket. The radio played in the background, and Mickey's head bobbed in time to the music as she ate. She took a sip of her drink.

"Chocolate milk shakes go great with pizza," she said.

"I've always thought so," Deanna agreed. "They also go great with cheeseburgers and chips."

Mickey grinned at her. "Let's have that tomorrow."

"Maybe we should cook tomorrow."

"Let's cook cheeseburgers," Mickey said, and giggled. "I like junk food."

Deanna held up her slice of pizza and examined it. "This doesn't look junky to me." As she took a bite, a strand of cheese pulled away. "Mmm, gooey, though," she mumbled, and chased it with her tongue.

"So this is where you are."

Startled, both Deanna and Mickey looked up. Lee leaned against the doorway watching them, arms folded across his chest. He still wore his suit, but his tie and the top buttons of his shirt were undone. For once his eyes looked soft, and a smile played about his mouth.

Deanna swallowed hastily, then wiped her mouth with a napkin, very aware of his presence and how handsome he was when he smiled.

"Hello," she said a little self-consciously. "You're early."

He shrugged. "I finished sooner than I thought I would." He glanced around the room. "I see you two have been busy spending money."

There was a sudden, worried look in Mickey's eyes, and she put down her pizza. "Did we...did we buy too much stuff?"

"I wouldn't think so, Michelle," he said, then turned to Deanna as though to ask, *Did you?*

Deanna got up. "I kept the receipts," she said quietly, reaching into the pocket of her skirt. She handed him the papers. "I'm sure you'll find we bought only what Mickey needed—clothes and shoes—and a few things to make her feel at home in this house." She forced a bright smile and looked at Mickey. "I'm full. How about you?"

Still subdued, Mickey nodded.

"Then let's get this cleaned up. I'll put the leftovers in the fridge if you take the garbage out." Ignoring Lee, she picked up the pizza box. "Do you want the rest of your milk shake?" she asked Mickey.

The girl shook her head. "I'm not hungry anymore. Should I take all these bags outside, too?" she asked.

"That sounds like a good idea," Deanna said. She went to the doorway. "Excuse me," she said coldly.

Her shoulder brushed against Lee's chest as she pushed past him.

She caught a drift of his musky after-shave, and awareness flickered along the perimeters of her anger. She refused to acknowledge it.

Damn him, she thought angrily. Why couldn't he have come home with a smile and a pleasant comment to Mickey about her room, her haircut—anything! The poor kid was full of doubts now, worrying that they'd spent too much money, worried that she was somehow a bother to her uncle.

Deanna suspected that Mickey was picking up on her uncle's unconscious signals. He *did* resent the girl's presence to a certain degree, Deanna was sure of it.

Lee came into the kitchen as she was wrapping the leftover pizza and stood in the doorway watching her. He had taken off his suit jacket and tie and rolled up the sleeves of his shirt. He looked tousled and approachable—until she saw the coolness that was back in his eyes.

"I didn't mean to imply that you'd spent too much money," he said with a touch of stiffness.

Deanna closed the fridge door and turned. "I'm not worried about myself," she said, frowning. "But you upset Mickey. It's pretty obvious that she and her mother didn't have any money to spare, and now she's afraid that you're going to be short. I think you should have a talk with her about it."

She saw his eyes narrow and his lips tighten as though he was about to tell her to mind her own business, but then Mickey came around the corner carrying a shopping bag stuffed full of garbage.

"That's all," she said, glancing at Lee. "Should I take it out to the back?"

"Your uncle will do it," Deanna said quickly. "You walk me to the door. It's time I was getting home." She took Mickey's hand, and as they passed Lee, she smiled sweetly. "You won't forget about that talk you wanted to have with her, will you, Mr. Stratton?"

She tapped the end of Mickey's nose with a finger. "Don't worry. You aren't getting a lecture. Your uncle just wants to fill you in a little on his finances, so you won't have concerns about money."

She shot Lee a defiant look. Family finances should be shared. Mickey needed to know that her uncle could afford to take care of her.

"Goodbye." Her smile for Lee was as falsely bright as the tone of her voice. Let him glare. With a haughty toss of her head, she left.

DEANNA WAS UP EARLY the next morning. She was sitting on the front steps sipping coffee and letting morning sun dry her hair into a cloud of reddish curls when she saw Lee and Mickey leave their house.

She sat up straighter as she waited for them to turn into her yard. Her smile for Lee was cool, but it warmed as she greeted Mickey.

"Hi, kiddo," she said. "How are you?"

"Pretty good," Mickey said, grinning up at her. "What are we gonna do today?"

"How about a picnic at the zoo?"

"Yeah! Can we have peanut-butter-and-banana sandwiches?"

Deanna made a face. "That's a pretty yucky combination." She sighed. "But if we must..."

"We must," Mickey said, then giggled. "Can I go see the cats?"

"Leo is on my bed. Alfie and Imp are in the backyard."

Deanna watched Mickey dash up the stairs and into the house, then turned to Lee as he was starting away.

"Just a minute," she said. "There's something I forgot to ask you about yesterday."

"I find that hard to believe," he said sarcastically.

Ignoring his tone and narrowed eyes, she went on, "There was nothing in Mickey's room from her old home—no doll or teddy bear, not even a picture of her mother. Surely you must have brought something back with you. It's important that she have some memento of her past. Her life didn't begin the day she moved in with you." Deanna tried to keep the accusation from her voice, but could tell from the look on his face that she hadn't succeeded.

He was glaring at her, obviously struggling to keep a rein on his temper. "I pay you to take care of Michelle's needs, not butt in."

"This *is* one of Mickey's needs," Deanna said stubbornly.

He drew a sharp breath. "Don't push it, lady or I'll..."

"Fire me?" she finished for him. She shook her head. "That would be a bad move and you know it." She returned his glare unwaveringly. "Look. Like it or not, Mickey is yours now and you'd better start thinking beyond her physical needs."

"Have you finished?" he asked through tight lips.

"For now," she said, holding her ground, hoping he *wasn't* perverse enough to fire her.

"Then remember that you were hired to baby-sit, not to practice Psychology 101," he said coldly. He glanced at his watch and frowned impatiently. "I'll be late tonight." And with that he turned on his heel and left.

Deanna watched him go, wishing she could throw something at that stiff, retreating back. Growling with frustration, she went into the house, slamming the door behind her.

Mickey was standing near the doorway to the kitchen, one of the kittens clutched to her chest.

Deanna groaned inwardly. How much had she heard?

"Are you and my uncle fighting?" she asked in a subdued voice.

"A bit," Deanna said honestly. There wasn't much point in pretending otherwise.

"Is it about me?"

Deanna shook her head. "No, Mickey. It isn't about you." That was true—it was about his attitude. "We didn't agree about something, that's all. It happens with adults sometimes."

Mickey nodded. "My mom and dad used to fight. I can remember. I didn't like it."

"Of course you didn't." They must have been bad fights, Deanna thought, for Mickey to remember them after all this time. "But your uncle and I only had a little argument, and it's all over with. Don't worry, sweetie, okay?"

Mickey shrugged, her cheek brushing against the cat's soft, black fur. "But... Uncle Lee's your boss, right?"

Deanna hated that idea. "I suppose he is."

"And if you fight with your boss, you could get fired, right?"

"I don't think your uncle will fire me," Deanna said. She smiled reassuringly at the girl and bent down to give her a quick hug. "Come on, kiddo—let's get some sandwiches made. Mornings are the best time to see the animals at the zoo. Go wash your hands and you can slice the bananas."

"Okay," Mickey said. She put down the cat and pulled a stool over to the kitchen sink to wash.

But Deanna saw the look of doubt on the girl's face and sighed inwardly. Mickey was right—Lee *could* fire her at any time. Neither she nor Mickey wanted that. She was going to have to try to stop being so confrontational, find another way to put her point across to him. But one way or another, she would. She could be stubborn about some things, and this was one of them. Mickey needed a loving home, and Deanna was determined that Lee Stratton give her one. Sooner or later he was going to have to pay less attention to his business and more to his niece.

DEANNA SAT on a lawn chair in her backyard. It was late evening and dark clouds were rolling in from the west, dimming the sun's lingering rays. Lightning flickered, then flashed. Thunder grumbled close behind. The air was thick with moisture.

"Deanna..."

Startled, she looked around. Lee stood just inside the gate at the bottom of the yard. She sat up straight, frowning slightly. What did he want?

"I thought I heard you talking to someone," he said, cutting across the lawn to where she was sitting. He was wearing shorts and an unbuttoned cotton shirt.

"Just the cats," she said lightly, watching him a trifle warily. She was tired. She didn't feel up to another confrontation. "What do you want?" she asked bluntly.

"May I sit down?"

"Of course." She gestured to the other chair. It was better than having him hover over her.

As he sat, Leo came to him, delicately sniffing at one of his long bare legs. The cat's ears flattened, and he disdainfully turned his back, tail twitching in irritation. Deanna had to smile.

"He doesn't like you."

"That's all right with me," Lee returned.

"Is Mickey okay?" she asked, wondering why he'd come over.

"She's sleeping."

Deanna glanced at the sky. As the storm approached, the wind quickened, stirring the leaves to frenetic rustling. "The storm may wake her up," she said. "You should be there in case she's afraid."

Lee frowned impatiently. "This isn't a social call. I won't be long."

"New orders?" she asked flippantly.

"Yes," he said, his frown deepening. "I'm going to California day after tomorrow. Is there any problem with your keeping Michelle while I'm gone?"

She shook her head. "It'll be fun." It would also be nice to know she wouldn't have to face him twice a day. "I enjoy her company." The wind whipped a strand of hair across her face. She tucked it behind her ear. "How long will you be away?"

"I can't say for sure. Four or five days, probably." He looked up at the sky. It was dark overhead and to the south, but brighter to the northwest where the sun was setting. "It looks like this might blow over."

"I hope not. We haven't had a decent thunderstorm all summer."

"Let me guess—you love storms."

A slap of lightning rode on his words and thunder followed with a crash. Deanna stood, raising her face to the splash of rain that followed. She looked down at him and laughed with excitement, forgetting for a moment the animosity between them.

"Isn't it wonderful?" She raised her face again, letting the rain pelt against it.

"I knew you were a witch," he murmured, getting to his feet. "You probably brought this on with a wave of your wand."

She grinned at him, her eyes sparkling. "It was the eye of newt and toe of toad that did it."

He returned her smile and stood beside her while the rain sluiced from the sky. The wind was deliciously cool, redolent with the odor of freshly washed earth. Lightning forked with purple-white tines, the flash lingering in their eyes. Thunder cannoned, shaking the ground.

Deanna turned to Lee, wiping the moisture from her eyes. "That was a big one."

Rain trickled over his face, and down his chest soaking the waistband of his shorts. She could see where it had darkened the fine gold hair on his legs and thighs. To her disquiet, she found herself staring. He was undeniably attractive. A sexy man. She looked up.

He was watching her, his eyes lingering where her wet dress, molded by the wind, clung to her skin. Quickly she looked away, feeling her heart trip a little faster.

She blinked, shaking water from curls that had tightened into a tangle of tiny ringlets—then felt his fingers, soft on her cheek as he brushed back a clinging lock of hair. The gentle touch was over before she could really react, but she could feel its imprint, its trace of warmth on her rain-cooled skin.

It was a struggle not to raise a hand to touch where he had touched. She glanced at him, her eyes wide with uncertainty.

"You'd better—"

"Get back to Michelle," he finished, examining her face closely. "I know." He hesitated for a moment, as though there was something he wanted to say. Then, with a shake of his head, he started toward the gate. Stopping, he looked back.

"Good night, Deanna," he said abruptly.

"Good night," she echoed as she watched him leave. She rubbed her palms over her upper arms, shivering slightly as he became a blur in the falling rain, then touched her cheek with the tips of her fingers. She sighed.

She'd had a niggling sense of attraction to him before. Tonight it had made itself felt.

She was thoroughly soaked now and beginning to get chilled, but she stood in the rain for a few moments longer, wondering at her reaction. Her attraction to him was only natural, she told herself firmly. She was a healthy young woman. Even though her heart was still with Ryan, it was inevitable that she would occasionally find another man attractive. It didn't mean anything, not really.

He had touched her. So what? A gentle touch, by no means sexual. But certainly far from impersonal... And his eyes had shown quite clearly that he'd felt something of what she did.

Okay. There might be a mutual attraction there, but it was strictly physical. They didn't even like each other.

Thoughtfully she went into the house, followed by Leo, who darted out from under a lawn chair, angry with the rain.

This had to be the first time she and Lee had parted without harsh words on one side or the other. All in all, it had been their least confrontational meeting yet. That should have felt good. Instead, it left her with an odd little feeling of disquiet. Something had changed.

CHAPTER FIVE

IF DEANNA HAD THOUGHT—hoped—things had changed between her and Lee, she was mistaken. She'd gone to his house this morning, instead of the other way around, and he had a decidedly preoccupied air. Wordlessly he handed her some money and left for California, his goodbye to Mickey a distracted afterthought.

Deanna caught a glimpse of the wistful look in Mickey's eyes as the door closed after Lee. Those two weren't any closer than they'd been when she'd first met them. Lee seemed to feel little beyond obligation toward Mickey, and Mickey knew it. It kept her quiet and subdued around him, preventing him from seeing what a bright and loving child she really was. It was all so disappointing.

Deanna tweaked a lock of Mickey's hair. "Well, kiddo, what do you want to do first? We can take a ride on one of the riverboats or go to the museum and planetarium."

Mickey shrugged, showing none of her usual enthusiasm for an outing. "I don't care," she said.

Deanna bent down and hugged her. "Maybe," she said, her cheek resting on Mickey's head, "we could just have a quiet day at home by the pool. How does that sound?"

Mickey's arms crept up around Deanna's neck and squeezed tight. "Okay," she said, her voice muffled. "You could read to me if you want."

"I'd like that." Deanna kissed her cheek, then stood. "I'll go home and get my bathing suit. You put yours on and meet me by the pool."

Nodding, Mickey started down the hallway, head hanging, walking slowly for once. *She needs so much to be loved,* Deanna thought with a now familiar pang, *to know she's really wanted.* Opening the door, she let herself out. It hadn't been so very different for her, growing up. Deanna always felt her parents' love came more from a sense of duty than any real feeling.

She'd disappointed them right from birth. She was a second child, her sister three years older. They had planned on a boy. The nursery was decorated in blue. The layette was blue. Deanna was not what they'd wanted. Before she was two, her mother gave birth to the desired son.

Maybe if she had taken after her parents, been a bright overachiever like her brother and sister, it would have been different. But she'd been a shy, rather awkward child, inclined to daydream. She'd spent much of her childhood lost in books, inventing imaginary worlds and people. While her sister went on to become a doctor and her brother a lawyer, she had dropped out of university before receiving her degree.

They might have considered her a success if she'd written a book critically acclaimed by Canada's literary elite. But a children's book—science fiction at that—didn't count as much of an achievement. Deanna wondered cynically if her parents ever mentioned it, even in passing. She knew for certain they hadn't read it and probably never would.

She let herself into her house and went to put on her bathing suit. She could empathize with Mickey's predicament, but her parents had loved her in their own way. She might have faced their disappointment, but never cold indifference. They might not have been able to give her all she needed, but they had never ignored her or refused her love.

Poor Mickey, she thought, pulling on her suit. What was going to become of her? How long would it be before she became sullen and withdrawn, started acting out? How would Lee respond then?

She sighed as she pulled a beach towel from the linen closet, thinking again of how Lee kept his distance from Mickey. Was there really any hope that the two of them could grow close, or was she just fooling herself when she thought she could help?

TWO DAYS AFTER Lee's departure, Deanna was in his kitchen making a light supper for herself and Mickey. Mickey was by the pool, reading.

Deanna glanced out the window and saw Mickey frowning in concentration as she turned the page. It was great to see how quickly she had taken to the adventures of Tasha Tran from the planet Plentitude, in spite of the reading level being a bit too high for her.

Deanna opened the fridge and took out the lettuce she'd picked earlier and started to make a salad, adding snow peas and baby carrots, also from her small garden. As she began to butter bread for sandwiches, the doorbell rang. Deanna pulled an oversize T-shirt on over her bathing suit and went to answer it.

A man stood on the doorstep, hands in the pockets of his jeans. He looked nervously at Deanna.

"Can I help you?" she asked cautiously.

"Uh, yeah. Is Lee home?"

"Not at the moment."

"When'll he be here?"

"I'm not sure exactly. It could be anytime now." She wasn't going to let this stranger know that Lee was out of the country.

"Are you, uh, his wife or something?"

"No. I look after his niece while he's at work."

"Mickey's here, then."

"Who are you?" Deanna asked bluntly, but she already knew. The dark hair, pale blue eyes and stubborn chin gave him away.

"Wade Wescott. I'm Mickey's father. I'd like to see her."

Oh, great, Deanna thought. After all these years, why did he have to show up now? Wishing Lee were here, she hesitated, not knowing what to do.

"She's my kid," Wade said. His chin thrust out and he scowled. "I got a right to see her if I want."

"Mickey hasn't seen you in years. I'm not even sure she'd know who you are. Maybe you should let me prepare her for this, Mr. Wescott. If you give me a number where you can be—"

"Deanna, what's this mean?" Mickey was coming down the hall, open book in hand. She held it up for Deanna to see, pointing to the troublesome word. "I can't figure it out."

As Deanna turned, Wade pushed the door open.

"Hey, Mick, is that you?" There was a pleased smile on his face. "You've really grown up, baby."

Frowning, Mickey stared at him. Deanna could see the puzzled look in her eyes change to one of cautious recognition. "Are you my dad?"

He grinned in delight. "I sure am. How you been?"

Deanna watched Mickey. Her thin face went pale and still, her pale blue eyes wide as she stared at her father. "Mom died," she said in a small voice.

Wade squatted down and put a tentative hand on his daughter's shoulder. "I heard, baby. Family services found me and told me. That's why I came. I'm real sorry."

Mickey stood stiffly under his touch. She might have recognized him as her father, but too much time had passed for her to have any ready feeling for him.

Gently Deanna pulled Mickey to her side, holding her protectively. She felt the tense little body relax against her.

"Mr. Wescott, this has been a bit of a shock for Mickey. Maybe we should take it slowly."

Wade straightened up and looked at her. For a moment, Deanna thought he was going to argue.

"All right," he said reluctantly. He looked back at Mickey. "I'll see you tomorrow, Mick. Okay?"

Mickey pressed closer to Deanna. "Okay," she said in a subdued voice. She stood still and watched her father leave.

Deanna waited until he had climbed into his car, an old model with faded green paint and a good deal of rust, before closing the door. She bent down to take Mickey into her arms, hugging her close. Mickey sighed tremulously.

Deanna stroked her hair. "How do you feel, sweetie?"

Mickey shrugged, but said nothing.

Deanna pushed back a bit and looked into her face, smiling gently. "A little mixed-up?"

Mickey nodded, her eyes filling with tears. "I thought I'd be all glad to see him, but..." Her voice broke and she drew a sobbing breath.

"But you don't really know him, do you?"

Mickey shook her head. "I almost didn't even know who he was."

Deanna brushed a strand of hair from Mickey's cheek. "It's all a little bit scary right now, isn't it?"

Mickey sighed and nodded. "Kinda. What am I gonna do?"

Deanna gave her a quick squeeze and stood up, keeping one hand on her shoulder. "Well, to start with, you can visit with your father and get to know him again. Would you like that?"

"I guess. Do I...do I have to go live with him?"

"No one is going to make you do anything you don't want to do. Right now your home is with your uncle."

"I think he might be glad if I went and lived with my dad."

"Not unless it's what you really want, Mickey. I'm sure of that." But she wasn't sure at all. Mickey could be right. Lee might be delighted if she chose to live with her father.

She felt a shiver run through Mickey's body. "Why don't you get out of that wet bathing suit, sweetie? Take a shower to warm up a bit. I'll have some supper ready for you when you come out."

"Okay," Mickey said dejectedly. The book bumped against her leg as she went down the hall, a forlorn figure with drooping head and slumped shoulders.

Deanna waited until she heard the shower in the main bathroom running, then went to phone Lee.

When she was put through to his hotel suite, a woman with a cheery, drawling voice answered the phone. She informed Deanna that Lee was in a meeting and offered to take a message.

"Tell him that Mickey's father is here," Deanna said, wishing she could have spoken directly to Lee. "I really need to talk to him," she added. "Could you please see that he gets the message as soon as possible?" Thanking the woman, she hung up the receiver, rubbing her thumbnail across her bottom lip.

She wondered for a moment who the woman on the other end of the line had been, then decided that Lee had probably hired—or taken—someone to assist him. Visions of him having a fling with some blond beach bunny were quickly dismissed. It was a business trip, after all, and Lee, she was sure, would be all business.

She just hoped he phoned back soon. She had no idea what she was supposed to do.

LEE HADN'T RETURNED her call by noon the next day, and Deanna assumed that meant he wasn't all that concerned about Wade's presence. While she was disappointed that he couldn't be bothered to discuss the situation with her, it just reinforced what she had believed all along. He didn't really care about his niece. Maybe it was just as well Mickey's father *had* come back into her life. True, he hadn't had any contact with her for years, but Deanna didn't know the whole story. Perhaps Mickey's mother had made it hard for him to keep up the relationship. Now, it seemed, he was ready to rectify the situation. Better late than never, she thought.

When Wade Wescott finally showed up that afternoon, Deanna invited him to join her and Mickey at the pool, hoping she was doing the right thing.

Still subdued and withdrawn, Mickey returned her father's greeting quietly. She sat huddled in a deck chair, one of the black cats curled up beside her. Deanna had let her bring the kittens over, knowing they provided some comfort. At this point, she really didn't care if Lee minded or not. Mickey came first.

"Would you like something to drink?" she asked Wade as he took a seat across from Mickey.

"Uh, yeah, sure. Beer, if you got it."

"I don't think we do. How about a soft drink?"

He shrugged and smiled pleasantly enough. "As long as it's cold, I guess."

Returning with the drinks, Deanna saw that Wade had inched his chair closer to Mickey's. He was leaning forward, his elbows resting on his knees while he chatted affably to his daughter.

He didn't seem a bad sort, Deanna thought, putting his drink down on the table beside him. His clothes looked a bit shabby and his hair needed cutting, but he had a certain charm. Deanna could see Mickey slowly warming to him. Good, she thought, sitting down quietly. Maybe this was just what Mickey needed.

Wade picked up his drink and took a long swallow. He made a face as he put the can down. "Well, it isn't beer, but it's better than nothing in this heat. Hey, Mick, what d'you say? Want to go for a swim?'' He jerked a thumb toward the pool. ''Might as well use it while you've got it.''

''I guess.'' Mickey carefully put the cat down and got up, tugging at the bottom of her bathing suit. She went to the pool and sat on the edge, dangling her feet in the cool, blue water.

Wade stood and stripped off his T-shirt, then took his wallet and keys from the pockets of his cutoffs. He sauntered around the edge of the pool to the diving board, then jumped into the water with a great splash. Surfacing, he tossed his head back.

''Whew-ee! That feels great! C'mon, Mick, jump in!''

Mickey hunched her shoulders and shook her head.

Deanna watched her and her father. Was there a chance, given a bit of time, that the two of them could form a real bond? She had the impression that Wade wanted his daughter. Would Lee let her go? Would he have any choice? Surely Wade's claim to Mickey was stronger.

Bending her head to one side, she raked her fingers through her hair to hasten its drying. Whatever the outcome, she hoped, for Mickey's sake, it could all be resolved peacefully.

As the supper hour approached, Wade showed no sign of leaving. Deanna debated for a moment, then asked him if he would like to stay for the meal. He accepted with haste, confirming her suspicion that he had been hoping for the invitation.

''I'm starved,'' he said, picking up Mickey's towel and wiping it across his face. ''Whatcha got?''

''I was planning on hot dogs. Barbecued.''

He made a face. ''Tube steaks, eh? I'd rather have the real thing. Well, I guess it'll do.''

You're darned right it will, Deanna thought as she turned away. She was beginning to find him a bit loud and brash.

It's Mickey's feelings that count here, she told herself firmly, *not yours.* Wade might not be as polished as Lee, but if he could give his daughter some genuine love and affection, then that was all that mattered.

"STILL NO BEER, huh?" Wade said as he accepted a frosty glass of lemonade from Deanna. He took a sip, then grimaced. "Too much of this stuff could be deadly."

"I'd be happy to make tea or coffee if you'd rather," Deanna said, keeping her tone neutral."

"In this heat? Thanks, but no thanks." He grinned with obviously practiced charm, as though he realized Deanna's growing irritation.

Turning her back on him, Deanna went to the barbecue and took the weiners off the grill. "Supper's ready, Mickey," she called to the girl.

Mickey put the cat she'd been holding down and got up slowly. "I'm not very hungry," she said.

Deanna pulled her close for a quick hug. "I know it's hard to eat when it's so hot. But try and get a few mouthfuls down, sweetie. You'll feel better if you do."

"I s'pose." She took her plate from Deanna and went to sit at the patio table across from her father. Picking up the ketchup bottle, she added a healthy dollop to her hot dog.

"Pass me that, Mick," Wade said, holding out his hand. "I need something to kill the taste."

In spite of the fact that she wanted to like the man, Deanna was growing more annoyed with him with each passing moment. Still, she held her tongue, not wanting to upset Mickey.

Taking her own plate, Deanna went to join them. She wasn't all that hungry herself and merely nibbled at her food. Wade, she noticed, wolfed his down and reached for more, looking as though he hadn't eaten in a while.

"Where do you work?" she asked him.

He shot her a quick look. "I'm working for the government right now," he said, and winked. "The unemployment division. Pay's lousy, but the hours are great."

Deanna gave a noncommittal smile. "What did you do before?"

"Worked here and there," he said with a shrug. He took a mouthful of food and spoke around it. "Nothing to get excited about."

"Here in Winnipeg?"

He swallowed and shook his head. "I was up in Yellowknife—thought I'd try the North for a while. That's where I was when I found out about—" He stopped and glanced at Mickey. "You know."

Deanna glanced at Mickey, too, but the child wasn't listening. Alfie and Imp sat like twin shadows under the table, waiting patiently while Mickey sneaked them bits of her hot dog. If she took too long between bites, one of them would gently tap her leg with a paw to hurry things along. Deanna smiled, then turned back to Wade.

"I suppose you must be anxious to find a job," she said.

"If something interesting turns up, fine. If not . . . well, a good long holiday never hurt no one. I sure could use a place to stay, though."

Deanna was conscious of a hint behind the words. "Where are you staying now?"

"Some guy I met up North. We worked together for a couple of years. His wife's getting bitchy about it, though, sniping at him all the time. Don't know why he puts up with her."

Deanna didn't blame the woman. A little bit of Wade Wescott went a long way. What charm he did have wore thin fast.

Wade looked at her speculatively. "How about I stay here for a few days? Mickey would like it, wouldn't you, baby?"

"I'm sorry, but I can't let you stay," Deanna said before Mickey could respond. "Not without Lee's permission."

"Yeah, well, he'd never go for it. He's had it in for me ever since me and Teri got together—didn't think I was good enough for his precious little sister."

There was anger in his voice. Mickey was watching him, her eyes huge in her sun-flushed face.

"That was a long time ago," Deanna said hastily. She didn't want Mickey to have to listen to her father's diatribe against her uncle. "It doesn't matter now. You know, I'm sure you could find a room to rent somewhere nearby. It wouldn't cost much, and you'd still be close to Mickey."

"Yeah, I guess it would do. How about it, Mick?"

Mickey gave him a shy, sidelong look. "I s'pose," she said.

"Yeah. We could do some stuff together, go to the zoo and things. Betcha haven't been to the zoo in years, eh? We could feed the monkeys. Sound good, baby?"

Mickey glanced at Deanna, then back at her father. "You're not supposed to feed the monkeys," she said.

He shrugged. "So who'd know?"

"They could get sick," said Mickey. "But we could feed the ducks," she added hastily. "They have machines that you put in a quarter and get food for them."

"Sure, okay. So, it's a date, then. One of these days, we go to the zoo." Without committing himself to a specific time, he turned to Deanna and grinned. "I could go for another hot dog."

Deanna pushed the plate toward him. "Please," she said. "There's no point in throwing them away."

When he'd finished, Deanna began to stack dishes onto a tray to take back into the kitchen. Mickey and her father would open up a bit if she wasn't there. Normally she was a fairly talkative child, and her silence all afternoon had been unnerving. Deanna could only imagine what thoughts were running through her mind.

Deanna put the tray down on the kitchen counter, reveling in the air-conditioning. Under her bright pink T-shirt, her bathing suit was still damp and sticking uncomfortably to her skin. She tugged at the bottom to straighten it, then looked critically at her legs. The sunscreen seemed to have worked. There was no sign of a burn among the dusting of freckles. Shoving back a springy lock of hair, she started to load the dishwasher.

She was wiping off the counters when she heard a sound behind her. Startled, she turned around, dishcloth in her hand. Lee stood in the entrance way between the kitchen and dining room watching her.

There was an odd look in his eyes, the same look she had seen in them during the thunderstorm. Her heart skipped a beat, and she stared back, nervously nibbling her bottom lip and wondering at her involuntary reaction.

"You're home," she said, keeping her voice steadily neutral. "I didn't expect you for at least another day." He looked tired. Hadn't the meetings been successful?

"We wound things up last night—early morning, actually." He came into the kitchen and pulled a stool out from under the breakfast counter. Sitting down, he wrapped his legs around the rungs and leaned forward on his elbows. His eyes, hooded and lazy, roamed over her.

"You're staring," she accused.

His laugh was low and surprisingly warm. "I was just thinking it's nice to come home and find a half-clad nymphet making my supper. I could get to like this."

"Mickey's supper," Deanna corrected, hiding a smile. "And we've already eaten." She added a stern note to her voice. "I might have been persuaded to make you something if it wasn't for that nymphet remark. Any more of that nonsense and you eat out—alone."

He laughed again, his eyes crinkling at the corners. He seemed infinitely more approachable. More attractive. Deanna had to look away.

"Where's Michelle?" he asked.

"She's outside with her father."

Lee's face went still. He straightened, staring at her in disbelief. "Her father? Wescott's here?"

Uh-oh, Deanna thought, rubbing at a spot in the sink. "Yes. He showed up yesterday."

"Why the hell didn't you let me know?"

Deanna turned around, her eyes flashing. "I did! I called you and left a message with some woman for you to phone back. When I didn't hear from you, I assumed you didn't care. He came over today and I asked him to stay for supper."

Lee pushed back the stool and stood up. "I don't want that man in my home," he said through gritted teeth.

"How was I supposed to know what you wanted? You should have phoned and told me!"

"I didn't get your damned message. Are you sure you called?" His tone said clearly he didn't believe she had.

Deanna threw down the dishcloth and crossed her arms over her chest. "I called," she said, her lips tight with anger. "Check your phone bill at the end of the month, if you don't believe me. Besides, I didn't see any problem with him being here. Mickey seemed to want it. When I didn't hear from you, I assumed it was okay."

"You assumed a hell of a lot, lady. I don't want that man near Michelle."

"But…he's her father!" Deanna objected. "What harm can it do for her to see him?"

Without answering, Lee turned on his heel and headed for the door. He flung it open and strode outside. Deanna followed quickly.

Wade had pulled his lounge chair into the sun and was lying back with his eyes closed, arms folded behind his head. Mickey was sitting on the edge of the pool, slowly kicking the water. She glanced over her shoulder when she heard the door close behind Deanna.

Wade opened his eyes and spotted Lee. Moving lazily, he stretched and sat up. "Well, if it isn't Wonder Boy, home from the money wars," he said with sneering insolence.

"I was wondering how long it would take for you to turn up," Lee said coldly.

Wade got to his feet. "I had to make sure you're treating my kid right."

"She's mine now, Wescott," Lee said tightly. "The law says so."

Wade took a step closer to Lee, his jaw jutting belligerently. "Yeah? Well, maybe we'll see about that."

Lee's mouth twisted in arrogant challenge. "Go ahead. No court will ever turn her over to an unemployed drunk with no home to give her."

A flush of anger colored Wade's face and his hands bunched into fists. "I'm her father." His voice rose. "That gives me rights."

Deanna could feel the aggression flowing between the two men. It unnerved her, left her speechless, and she could do nothing but watch and hope their confrontation wouldn't go beyond words.

"You have no rights as far as Michelle is concerned." Lee's jaw was clenched with anger. "Not anymore. You gave those up a long time ago. Now, get your things together and get the hell—"

"Stop it! Just stop it!" Mickey stood beside the pool, her thin little body tense and shivering. "Don't fight!" Her face was pale and her eyes huge as she looked wildly from one man to the other. She let out a deep, shuddering breath. "Don't fight," she repeated, holding her arms tight against her stomach. She heaved suddenly, then gagged. With a panicked look at Deanna, she ran to the house, hand cupped over her mouth.

Deanna turned on the men. "You two are disgusting," she said coldly. Pivoting on her heel, she raced after Mickey.

She found her in the bathroom, hunched over the toilet, retching violently.

"Poor baby," Deanna murmured in heartfelt sympathy. She held her, stroking her back soothingly.

"I'm sick," Mickey said after a moment, looking up with tear-filled eyes.

"You sure are," Deanna said, placing a hand on the girl's brow. Mickey was shivering and her lips had a bluish tinge, but her skin felt warm to the touch. "Come. Let's get you cleaned up and into bed."

After washing her quickly, Deanna led her to her room and helped her out of her damp bathing suit and into pajamas. Still shivering, Mickey crawled into bed and pulled the covers up around her. Deanna sat on the edge of the mattress, gently stroking her forehead.

"You'll warm up in a minute," she said. "If not, I'll run next door and get my hot-water bottle for you to cuddle. Now. Do you think you'll be sick again?"

Mickey made a pained expression and nodded briefly. "My stomach's all yucky."

"I'll go find a basin, then, so you won't have to worry about making it to the bathroom. Will you be all right for a couple of minutes?"

Mickey nodded. She sighed and her eyes closed. Bending over, Deanna dropped a light kiss on her cheek, then went quietly from the room, closing the door behind her.

Lee was standing in the hall. "How is she?" he asked.

Deanna let all the anger and disappointment she was feeling come through. "How do you think she is after seeing you two fighting over her like dogs over a bone? She's sick, Lee, and damned upset. Don't you think she's been through enough? She doesn't need this on top of everything else.'' She brushed passed him and made her way to the kitchen.

There was a plastic basin under the sink. Taking it out, she slapped it onto the counter, then filled a glass with water and headed back to Mickey's room. Ignoring Lee, she took a deep breath to calm herself before pushing open the door.

Mickey lay huddled beneath the blankets. Every few seconds, a shudder ran through her body. Deanna placed the basin within easy reach and put the glass of water on the nightstand. She sat on the bed and gently brushed the hair back from Mickey's face.

''You're not feeling any better, are you kiddo?''

Mickey shook her head. ''I'm cold, Deanna.''

''I'll get that hot-water bottle. Will you be all right while I'm gone?''

Mickey sighed. ''Uh-huh. But hurry.''

''I will. Back in a sec.''

Lee was standing in the doorway. Deanna studied him for a long moment. Underlying the worry on his face was a look of shame. Deanna was glad to see it. He should never have expressed his anger at Wade in front of Mickey.

She motioned him out of the bedroom and closed the door behind them. ''She's feeling chilled,'' Deanna said. ''We should take her temperature—do you have a thermometer?''

''There's one in the medicine cabinet in my bathroom. I'll get it.''

''Okay. How about a hot-water bottle?''

He shook his head.

''I'll go get mine, then. You can take her temperature while I'm gone.''

Lee's lips twisted wryly. "Are you sure she'll let me near her?"

"Of course she will. I'll be back in a minute." She left quickly. Once outside, she glanced around, looking for Wade's car. It was nowhere in sight. Somehow it came as no surprise to learn that the man hadn't bothered to wait to see how his daughter was. Lee might be far from being the ideal guardian for Mickey, but he beat Wade hands down.

While she waited for the kettle to boil, she changed from her bathing suit and T-shirt into a soft denim skirt and blouse, then tugged a pick through her unruly hair. Leo had awakened from one of his prolonged naps and scratched at the door to be let out, tail twitching impatiently. She opened it, thinking she would have to retrieve the kittens from next door. She hoped they weren't digging holes in the flower beds. She didn't need Lee sniping at her over that. Then she filled the hot-water bottle and hurried back next door.

She could hear the sound of Mickey retching as she entered the house. "Oh, no," she murmured, hurrying down the hall to the bedroom.

Lee was sitting on the edge of the bed, supporting Mickey while she was sick. When at last Mickey gave a sobbing sigh and flopped back on the pillow, Deanna could see the worry on his face.

She went into the bathroom for a facecloth, then returned and handed it to Lee.

"Wipe her face while I empty the basin," she said, keeping her voice soft.

Mickey's eyes were closed. As Lee touched the facecloth to the corners of her mouth, she opened her eyes and stared at him.

"I'm sorry," she said, her eyes filling with tears.

"There's nothing for you to feel sorry about," Lee said firmly. "You've got a touch of the flu, that's all. You'll probably be fine tomorrow. Try and rest now."

With her eyes wide and blinking, Mickey stared at her uncle, then turned her head as Deanna came over with the basin and hot-water bottle.

"Are you still chilled, kiddo?" Deanna asked.

"A bit."

"Hold this, then," Deanna said, handing her the hot-water bottle, wrapped in a towel. "It should warm you up."

Mickey took it and held it to her chest. A shudder ran through her. "Thanks," she whispered. Her eyes fluttered shut.

Lee got up slowly and went to the door, inclining his head for Deanna to follow.

"What's wrong with her?" he demanded as soon as they were clear of the room.

"Probably just the flu. Although," she went on, giving him a frowning glance, "it could have something to do with that display you and her father put on out there."

"You're repeating yourself," he said, frowning back at her. "Should we call a doctor?"

"Do you have a pediatrician for her?"

"Uh, no."

"Then call a clinic and talk to one of the doctors. I'm going to go sit with her until she falls asleep."

Let Lee handle it. It was time for him to take on more than a financial responsibility for his niece. She opened the bedroom door and slipped back inside.

She sat carefully on the edge of Mickey's bed. As she laid a gentle hand on her brow, the girl murmured something but didn't open her eyes.

Deanna sat for a few moments until she was sure Mickey was asleep, then quietly left the room.

Lee was hanging up the phone when she came into the kitchen.

"Well?" she asked, pulling out a stool and sitting down.

"Like you said, probably the flu. She's to have lots of rest and fluids, and we're to keep her temperature down."

We? Deanna thought. She swung one leg gently back and forth as she looked at Lee. "You know, she's probably going to be sick off and on through the night. These things usually last several hours."

Lee flopped down on a stool opposite her, stretching out his legs. "Damn," he muttered under his breath.

Deanna felt a flash of irritation. "Yes. It's all very inconvenient for you. You're just too busy for this. Well," she said, standing up, "don't worry. I'll look after her—and I won't even charge extra for it." She stalked angrily from the room.

Lee caught up to her in the hallway. He put a hand on her shoulder. "That wasn't what I meant, damn it."

Frowning angrily, Deanna shrugged him off. "No? That's the message I've been getting all along. Mickey, too, for that matter."

He sighed tiredly and rubbed the back of his neck. "I know I haven't spent enough time with Mickey, but things have been pretty hectic with the business. This last deal was the biggest one we've ever attempted. It's turned everything around and paved the way for us to go international. I had to keep at it, even after I heard my sister, Teri, was dying."

A flash of pain darkened his eyes and he sighed again. "I just couldn't stop things. Business doesn't wait for personal problems to sort themselves out, and no one else was in a position to take over. My two partners are the creative force. I'm the businessman. They were counting on me. I had to keep going. But it's over now, except for the paperwork."

Deanna was leaning against the wall, arms crossed. She felt herself softening. "Does this mean you'll have more time to spend with Mickey?"

"I have to go into the office tomorrow to finish up a couple of reports, then I'm going to take some time off."

"Good." She tilted her head to one side and looked at him. "So... am I out of a job?"

"No." He hesitated for a moment. "I thought it might make things easier for Mickey if you were around, too. If that's all right with you, of course," he finished a little stiffly.

Deanna kept back a smile. She liked seeing him hesitant and unsure of himself. "I don't know," she said slowly. "What would you expect from me?"

He shrugged. "Pretty much what you're doing now. I'd just... tag along, I guess." His sudden smile chased the arrogance from his face.

"I like going to the zoo, too," he added, laughter glinting in his eyes.

Deanna stared at him, surprised at just how much his smile affected her. She would have said yes right away if she hadn't felt that unnerving tug of attraction. As it was, she wanted to say no, tell him he was on his own, that she had given them enough of her time—but for Mickey's sake she couldn't. What he was suggesting would make things easier for Mickey, and that was the important issue. Still, she hesitated, wondering how she herself would feel having Lee around.

"Of course I would continue to pay you," Lee said, as though that was the reason for her hesitation. His voice had stiffened. The remoteness was back in his eyes.

Deanna started to tell him that money would have little to do with her decision. "That's not—" She stopped and shook her head. Maybe it was better this way. It kept a sense of business between them. "I'll do it," she said slowly.

"Good." His voice was cool. "Now—" A sudden moan and sounds of retching from Mickey's room stopped him. He pushed open the door and looked in.

Mickey was sitting up in bed, tears streaming down her face. "I'm sorry," she wailed. "I missed the basin. I couldn't help it."

Deanna went to her side. "Of course you couldn't," she said soothingly. "It's all right."

"B-but—" She stopped on a hiccuping sob and stared at her uncle. "I'm sorry!"

"It couldn't be helped, Michelle. Don't worry about it." He sounded calm and reassuring. "Deanna, take her into my bed. I'll change the sheets."

Deanna put an arm around Mickey. "Come on, sweetie. Let's change your pajamas and get you tucked in again. And it's okay. You can't help being sick."

After getting Mickey into clean pajamas and washing her flushed face, Deanna led her down the hall to Lee's room and pushed open the door.

She'd resisted the temptation to look into his room before, though she had been curious.

It was a large room with a pale gray carpet and black lacquered furniture. A burgundy and navy blue patterned comforter covered the king-size bed. There was a bathroom to one side, and patio doors opened onto the cedar deck. A modular unit filled one wall, its shelves bare except for a row of reference books alongside a small television set and sound system. There was a black leather chair and footrest next to a glass-topped chrome table scattered with computer magazines.

As Deanna pulled back the comforter and lifted the crisp sheet for Mickey to crawl under, she caught the faint musky scent she had come to associate with Lee. Involuntarily her nostrils flared and she breathed deeply.

Mickey lay back on the pillow, looking tiny and very young in the big bed.

"Deanna, what if I get sick *here?*" Her eyes brimmed with horror at the thought.

Deanna smiled reassuringly. "Just try and hit the basin—and if you miss, you miss. We'll change the bedding. Your uncle won't be upset, Mickey. He knows you can't help being sick."

Mickey blinked tired eyes. "What if..." Her voice trailed off and she bit her bottom lip.

"Tell me, sweetie," Deanna said, gently stroking her forehead.

Mickey drew a deep breath and released it in a tremulous sigh. "What if I get real sick, like...like my mom and your husband?"

Deanna shook her head. "That's not going to happen, Mickey. The doctor says you've got the flu, that's all. You'll see—by morning you'll feel a lot better. I promise." She bent down and kissed her cheek. "Get some sleep now."

"Are you going to stay?"

"You bet." She gave her another kiss and stood up. "Sleep now." As she tucked the covers around Mickey, the girl's eyes drifted shut. Turning around, she saw Lee in the doorway holding clean sheets against his chest. She walked quietly toward him.

"She's sleeping now. With any luck she won't be sick again, at least not for a while." Deanna cast a look over her shoulder. "Poor little thing," she murmured. "She's worried that she might be sick like her mother was."

"I heard," Lee said, stepping aside to let her pass.

Deanna glanced at him. His eyes were dark and his face still.

"Deanna, are you...widowed?"

She looked away and nodded abruptly.

"I'm sorry," he said softly. He laid a hand on her shoulder. "I didn't know."

"It doesn't matter." She didn't want to answer the questions she knew he wanted to ask. Not now. "I'll make up Mickey's bed," she said, her voice brisk.

"I'll do it," he said, crossing the hall and going into Mickey's room. "Are you really spending the night?" he asked over his shoulder.

Deanna shrugged as she followed him into the room. "I promised I would. If I thought she'd sleep through, I wouldn't bother, but chances are she's going to be up and down all night. That's usually how it goes with kids. I'll lie on the bed with her—that way I'll be there if she needs me." She stopped suddenly and looked at him, a line dividing her brow. "That's all right with you, isn't it?"

"Would it make any difference if I said it wasn't?" he asked dryly.

Deanna grinned. "No, actually."

"I didn't think so. Feel free to stay. I'm sure Mickey will be a lot happier knowing you're here." He shook the folds out of the bottom sheet and began to drape it over the bed.

Deanna watched him for a moment, wondering if he was being sarcastic. Deciding she'd heard no edge to his words, she went to help him.

She grabbed a corner of the sheet and tugged it to fit over the mattress. On the other side of the bed, Lee did the same, head bent as he smoothed creases from the sheet.

Deanna moved slowly, watching him. He still looked tired, but seemed more relaxed. He had taken off his tie and rolled up the sleeves of his dress shirt. Gold-brown hair scattered over his forearms down to his wrists. His hands were long and lean, his fingers square-tipped. Nice hands, the kind she liked. Suddenly the intimacy of their task struck her.

It seemed strange to be making a bed with him, someone she scarcely knew and didn't particularly like. Or did she?

The thought stayed with her as they finished. She might not have liked him much to start with, but now...

She watched as he stretched a bit and rubbed his neck. His eyes looked tired. Lines she hadn't noticed before fanned from their outer corners.

"I'm going to run home for a moment," she said. "I need a couple of things."

He nodded. "I'll be in with Mickey."

DEANNA LET HERSELF into her house, stooping to stroke Leo's head as he brushed passed her. She went slowly up the stairs to her room, lost in thought.

There was a change in Lee tonight. He was definitely more approachable. She'd have thought Mickey's illness would have caused him to turn away in disgust, but instead, he had been surprisingly gentle and understanding.

More so than Mickey's father would have been, Deanna realized. If Wade had really cared, he would have stayed until he knew Mickey was all right, no matter how angry Lee was.

Deanna sat on the bed, the cat jumping up beside her. Ears flat, he rubbed his head against her hand. Obligingly, she scratched. "Silly puss," she murmured absently.

She glanced at Ryan's picture and felt her stomach give a funny little twist. She had loved him so much, grieved so terribly when he died. In all the time since, she had never wanted another man.

She scowled suddenly, shaking her head. "And you don't now," she told herself firmly. She stood, dislodging the cat, who jumped to the floor with a disgruntled flick of his tail.

Lee Stratton might cause a spark of attraction to flare. She could accept that. It wasn't realistic to think she didn't have certain physical needs. But that didn't mean she had to act on them. She'd experienced real love, and she had beautiful memories. She wouldn't tarnish them.

No one else could give her what Ryan had, and she would never love anyone the way she'd loved him. And she could never accept anything less.

CHAPTER SIX

DEANNA DROPPED her small overnight bag just inside Mickey's bedroom and walked quietly down the hall to Lee's room. She stopped in the doorway and peeked inside.

Lee sat on the edge of the bed, staring down on a sleeping Mickey. His face was still, as though carved from stone, and his eyes were glazed. He blinked suddenly and took a deep breath. Tentatively he touched the tips of his fingers to Mickey's forehead, then stroked it lightly, briefly.

Deanna felt a little glow of satisfaction. It was the first time she had seen Lee touch his niece as though he cared about her. Maybe Mickey wouldn't have to go through life feeling lonely and rejected, after all. She pushed open the door.

"Hi," she said softly, then stopped, her mouth gaping in surprise. Curled on the bed were Alfie and Imp. "You let them in?" she asked Lee in disbelief. "And on your bed?"

"I don't mind cats," he said a little sheepishly. "In small numbers. They were sitting outside on the deck, and well, I thought Mickey might like having them here."

"I'm sure she will," Deanna agreed. That Lee Stratton would allow cats in his house, never mind on his bed, was the last thing she would have expected. "How is she?"

"She hasn't been sick since you left." He got up slowly, rubbing his neck. "And now that you're here, I'd like to shower and change."

"Of course," she said. "You look tired."

"I am. It's been a long day. No—I take that back. It's been like this for weeks now. Everything seemed to happen at once. I feel as though I haven't had time to look after anything properly." He glanced down at Mickey. "Least of all her."

Her lingering resentment and anger began to melt when Deanna saw the concern in his eyes. She felt another flash of hope for Mickey and gave him a quick smile.

"Go have your shower," she urged. "I'll be here if she wakes up."

With an abrupt nod, Lee turned and went into the adjoining bathroom, shutting the door behind him.

Deanna stared thoughtfully at the closed door. No doubt about it—there was a change in Lee's attitude. Things were starting to look rosier for Mickey.

Unless her father threw a spanner in the works, Deanna thought suddenly. Frowning, she went to sit on the edge of the bed, looking down on the sleeping child.

She had no remaining doubts about Wade's lack of suitability as a parent. It hadn't taken long before his company had begun to chafe and his flaws to show. The fact that he didn't have a steady job seemed to suit him just fine. And if he really did have the drinking problem Lee had alluded to... No, Mickey was better off with her uncle.

Lee could give her stability. Once he had spent some time with Mickey, he would realize what a bright and endearing child she was. It wouldn't be long before he came to love her, not out of a sense of avuncular duty, but because she had won his heart.

"You'll do it, kid," Deanna murmured. Fondly she touched a soft, flushed cheek. One of the cats opened yellow eyes and watched her for a moment before yawning and settling back to sleep. Deanna smiled. Mickey would be glad to see them—and probably as surprised as she had been.

She got up off the bed and moved to the patio doors. They'd been left open, letting late-evening heat mingle with the coolness from the air conditioner. A light breeze stirred the shimmering surface of the pool and carried a faint scent of roses. From an ornamental cherry tree, a robin sang his last song of the day as the sun slid toward the horizon. Deanna leaned against the doorway, looking out.

The sound of running water had stopped. Hearing the bathroom door open, Deanna turned around.

Lee came into the room, toweling his hair. He wore a short white terry robe tied carelessly about his waist, leaving his long, leanly muscled legs bare.

Deanna knew she was staring, but for a moment it didn't seem to matter. She had seen him in less, standing in the moonlight beside the pool and again in the storm when rain had sluiced down his body, but there hadn't been this kind of intimacy. His eyes met and held hers. Then she averted her gaze, conscious that something of what she was feeling must show.

"Mickey's still asleep, I see," Lee said, but he was looking at her and not his niece, his expression unreadable.

Deanna nodded. "Best thing for her." Her voice was surprisingly steady. In spite of herself, she was watching him again. "I think maybe I'll go sit outside for a while," she said hurriedly.

He draped the towel over his shoulders and opened a dresser drawer. "I'll join you in a bit."

Deanna slid open the screen door and went outside onto the deck. She plopped down in a chair, rolling her eyes upward and shaking her head in disbelief. That spark of attraction she had vowed not to fan was finding its own fuel.

Lee joined her within a few minutes. He wore an old black T-shirt tucked into gray sweatpants worn thin with age. His feet were bare and his hair had dried soft and fine over his forehead, golden strands glinting in the last rays of sunlight. He took a chair across from her, sliding down wearily as he stretched his long legs. His eyes closed for a moment, then opened lazily.

"Nice evening," he said, looking around.

"And hardly a mosquito to be had," Deanna said lightly.

"Good. I was thinking of having part of the deck screened off but haven't had the time." He fell silent, his hands folded over his stomach, his eyes half-closed.

"Tell me about your sister," Deanna asked softly, impulsively.

"Teri." For a moment, she wondered if he would say anything more, then he began to speak.

"She was six years younger than me. We were quite close when we were children, especially after our mother died. Dad was, well, not the best parent in the world, to put it mildly."

"Is he still alive?" Deanna interjected.

Lee nodded. "In Florida, last I heard. He's not one for keeping in touch—unless he wants something." There was resignation, not bitterness in his voice.

"Mickey didn't seem to think she had any family, except for you."

"I'm not surprised. Dad kicked Teri out when she was eighteen and pregnant. I tried my damnedest to talk her into coming to live with me, but she went straight to Wade. He dragged her from city to city, always looking for the easy way, never willing to work for what he wanted. He never held a job any longer than it took to qualify for unemployment insurance."

"Did you . . . were you and Teri still close?"

"Not by that time. We'd grown apart when we got older, and she knew how much I disapproved of Wade. We tried to get some of our earlier closeness back after she left him. We talked a lot on the phone. But whenever I suggested she come for a visit or I go see her, she put me off with one ex-

cuse or another. She did let me send her money once she realized she was never going to get any child support from
Wescott, but even that took quite a bit of convincing on my
part. I wanted them to come and live with me, but Teri refused to even consider it.''

''I guess she wanted to prove she could make it on her
own,'' Deanna said. She could understand.

''I suppose. And for the most part, she did, I think. She
seemed happy enough when I talked to her, and I really felt
she was beginning to get her life back on track. But there
were problems she didn't share with me until she was...until
she was dying.''

His voice tightened, but he went on, ''And she only told
me then because she wanted me to promise that Wade would
never get custody of Mickey.''

The thought of Wade's taking Mickey was not a pleasant
one. ''Does he have a chance? Legally?''

Lee sighed and rubbed a hand over his eyes. ''Not if I can
help it. I'll keep that promise to Teri no matter what. They
weren't married, and he's had no contact whatsoever with
Mickey for over four years. Teri named me guardian...
but I just hope like hell he never decides to fight it.''

''Why was Teri so adamant he not have her?''

''His life-style, his drinking...his violent temper.'' Lee's
jaw hardened. ''He used to beat Teri. But she stayed with
him until he began taking out his frustrations on Mickey. He
never actually hit Mickey, but Teri said she became convinced it would happen sooner or later. That's when she left.
I wish...''

''What?'' Deanna asked softly when he hesitated.

''That she hadn't been so damned independent, that she
had let me help. That she'd gone for treatment earlier.
Maybe then she'd—'' He stopped abruptly.

Deanna's eyes welled with tears of sympathy. "Oh, Lee—you don't know that things would have been different. And you can't blame yourself for the choices she made."

"No," he said slowly. "I suppose not. But I can keep my promise to give Mickey a good home and keep her safe from Wade. Although now that he's put in an appearance, I don't know how easy that's going to be."

"But surely if he drinks... and he did abuse Teri..." Deanna shook her head. "No one would let him have custody."

"There's no proof that he beat Teri. She never went to the police, and they moved around so much it would be impossible to find witnesses, especially after all this time. And as far as the drinking goes, all he has to do is say he's stopped and go to a few AA meetings. In fact, if he gets married and keeps a job for a while..." Lee's face was grim. "He *is* her father. A court could decide that he should have custody, and he's spiteful enough to try for it."

Deanna might have had her doubts in the past, but no longer. The best place for Mickey was with Lee. What she had seen earlier tonight convinced her that he did care, and what she had just heard confirmed her instincts that Wade didn't and never would.

"Well, we'll just have to make sure he doesn't succeed," she said.

"We?"

It was getting too dark to read his face clearly, but in her mind she could see his eyebrows rise haughtily over cool, green-flecked eyes. Maybe she had sounded a bit presumptuous, but still!

"After this afternoon—and from what you just told me—I think Mickey would be better staying with you. Especially now that you're going to..." She paused, not wanting to antagonize him. She liked the new footing they were on, tenuous though it was.

"Spend more time with her?" he finished easily enough.

"Well, yes. She's a wonderful little girl, Lee. And she needs so much to know she's loved and wanted." Deanna wished she could see his face clearly. His silence was unnerving. Had she gone too far again?

"I suppose you're right," he said finally, his tone neutral. "Maybe we should check on her." He got up to go inside.

Deanna followed, stopping just behind him as he opened the screen door. "I was thinking of making something to eat," she said. "I didn't get much supper. Would you like a sandwich?"

He turned. "Yes. Please. That would be nice."

"Any preferences?"

"Anything but peanut butter and banana," he said. Despite the deepening dusk, Deanna saw his mouth quirk in a smile.

Deanna nodded and smiled back, then went to the kitchen while he checked on his niece.

She thought about Lee, about how much more relaxed—and gentler—he seemed. It was a very appealing side of him, and it added to the attraction she couldn't deny she felt.

She paused with her hand on the refrigerator door, frowning, disturbed by the direction her thoughts persisted in taking. She wanted to like Lee, to feel comfortable in his company, which would ease things for Mickey.

She didn't want to feel attracted to the man. It could only complicate matters. With an impatient toss of her head, she opened the fridge and began to take out sandwich fixings, determined not to let her tenuous feelings for Lee develop further. Friendship was enough.

MICKEY SLEPT fairly peacefully for the first half of the night. She made up for it by waking up, sick, off and on until morning. Deanna slept when she could, huddled on the other side of Lee's bed. He had taken the spare room, rather than disturb Mickey.

Pearly light was stealing across the quiet city before Mickey fell into a deeper sleep. Deanna got up wearily to let the cats out into the yard, then stumbled back into bed. With any luck Mickey was over the worst of it. They could both use some uninterrupted sleep.

When Deanna woke again, she was alone in bed. The blinds had been drawn over the windows, but she could tell from the sun filtering through that it must be late. A glance at the clock on the bedside table told her it was almost eleven-thirty. She stretched, yawned, then curled up again, sleepily tucking the corner of the pillow under her cheek. It would have been easy to drift off again, but it was time to face the day. With effort, she rolled onto her back, then swung her legs over the edge of the bed. Yawning again, she ran her fingers through her tangle of hair.

She could hear the murmur of voices through the open patio door. Straightening her nightgown, she went to take a look, peering through the slats of the blind.

Lee sat back in one of the chairs, drinking from a mug and wearing a tolerant smile as Mickey chatted to him.

Mickey, still in her pajamas, sat cross-legged on the end of a lounge chair, dipping a spoon into a container of yogurt. For every spoonful she put in her mouth, one landed on the lid lying on the deck. The two black cats lapped it up, eyes half-closed in contentment.

Deanna smiled. She would take the time for a shower and give Mickey these moments with her uncle. Things were definitely looking up.

FRESH FROM HER SHOWER and dressed in a short denim skirt with a pale blue T-shirt, Deanna went outside to join them.

"Good morning," she said cheerfully.

Lee glanced at his watch and raised his eyebrows.

"Okay, okay, so it's afternoon." She sat down across from Mickey and grinned at her. "No need to ask—you're obviously over it."

"Yeah. I feel lots better." She shook her head. "I sure threw up a lot last night though. Hey—Alfie and Imp got to stay all night!"

"And have yogurt for breakfast. Weren't you hungry?"

Mickey shrugged. "Not like usual. But some. Uncle Lee was going to make me some French toast, but I said maybe later."

"How about you, Deanna?" Lee asked unexpectedly. "I thought I'd grab a bite to eat, then head for the office. I really need to be there for part of the day."

Deanna glanced at him. "Are you cooking?"

"I am."

"Then it sounds great. I am kind of hungry."

"Good. How about you, Mich—Mickey?"

"Um, maybe just a little bit, please."

"For you or the cats?" he asked, a teasing light in his eyes.

Mickey grinned. "Me."

"Okay, then. French toast it is. I'll call you when it's ready."

Deanna watched him go in through the kitchen door, not quite able to hide her look of surprise. Either Lee had changed overnight, or business pressures combined with grief—and a mingling of guilt—had hidden his true personality. It didn't matter, as long as the change was permanent. For Mickey's sake, she told herself firmly, glancing at the smiling girl.

"He's nice," Mickey said. "Nicer than before. He didn't even mind when I said to please call me Mickey, not Michelle." She made a little face. "I only get called Michelle when I've done something wrong."

"Well, Michelle . . ."

Startled, Mickey swung her head and stared at Deanna.

Deanna laughed and reached over to ruffle her hair. "Just teasing, sweetie. But why don't you go get dressed? Have a shower, too, if you feel up to it."

"Okay." Mickey jumped up and started toward the house. She stopped suddenly and turned, a worried look on her face. "Is . . . is my dad coming back?"

"I don't know, Mickey. But I do know that this is your home now. Your mom wanted Uncle Lee to take care of you, and that's what he's going to do. You don't have to go live with your dad."

Mickey sighed a little sadly. "Good. I mean, this is kinda strange still," she said waving a hand to the house and yard, "but it's the best I know right now. I want to be with you and Uncle Lee." Shoulders slumped, she went into the house.

With you and Uncle Lee. The words stayed with Deanna and she felt a twinge of uneasiness. She was a neighbor and a paid baby-sitter. No matter how fond she was of Mickey, she was in her life only temporarily.

It was a good thing Lee had decided to become more involved with his niece. The girl needed to realize her future was with him and him alone.

TWO DAYS LATER Deanna found herself seated in Lee's car and the three of them setting off for Lake Winnipeg.

Deanna settled back against the soft gray leather seat and looked out over the gleaming black hood. Not a paw print to be seen, she noticed, smiling.

Mickey, recovered from her brief bout of flu, wriggled with excitement under the restraints of her seat belt, chatting happily as the miles passed. Deanna shared some of her excitement. It seemed a long time since she had escaped the confines of the city.

It was a perfect day for the beach. They parked under a peach-leaf willow in the cooling shade cast by gnarled, reaching limbs. The air was thick with the scents and sounds of summer. An eastern kingbird perched pugnaciously in the top branches, and warblers darted to nests hidden in the tall grasses and cattails along the road.

After unpacking, they trudged up willow-studded dunes of fine white sand to the shore. Lake Winnipeg lay before them, as vast as an inland sea, its blue-gray waters stretching to the horizon.

"It's beautiful," Deanna murmured.

"And big!" Mickey said. She dropped what she was carrying and ran to the water's edge.

"I thought it would be more crowded," Lee said looking around. There were only a few small groups of people. "I guess most people go on to Grand Beach."

"Or to their cottages," Deanna said. "Anyway, it's nice it's not too crowded. I was at Grand Beach one time, and we could hardly move for all the baking bodies. Where shall we set up?"

"That way a bit. Away from the path. Mickey," he called, "come get your things. We're moving."

Mickey waved and trotted back. "This is a neat place!" she said enthusiastically. "Just like an ocean on TV or something. I never been to a place like this before. Are there crabs and things?" she asked her uncle as they walked on.

"No, this is fresh water. But there are some clams and sometimes crayfish, although I don't think you'll find any right around here. There are lots of sea gulls, though," he said, looking up. "And pelicans."

"Pelicans! The kind with those big, funny-looking beaks?"

Lee nodded, his eyes crinkling with laughter. "The same. I brought my binoculars. If I see any, I'll give you a call. How's this spot?"

"Perfect," Deanna said. She dropped her beach bag and umbrella on the sand and kicked off her sandals.

"Can I go swimming?" Mickey asked.

"Wait a sec," Deanna said. "Let me get some sunscreen on you." She rummaged in her bag for the container, then squeezed a dollop onto Mickey's thin shoulders.

"That's cold!" Mickey said, squirming while Deanna rubbed.

"It's better than frying. That sun would burn you to a crisp. There—that should do it. Away you go now."

Mickey needed no further bidding. She was off to the water.

Lee set up Deanna's beach umbrella, laying their brightly colored towels beneath it. He put the cooler with their drinks and sandwiches in the sparse shade of a bush near the dunes that formed the back of the beach.

Then he stripped off his shirt, so that he was wearing only navy shorts. His skin was smooth and lightly tanned, his bearing erect and confident. There was a taut leanness about him that implied hidden strength.

Deanna settled herself in the shade of the umbrella, studying him from behind her sunglasses. If he was aware of her eyes on him, he gave no sign as he stood watching Mickey splash in the water, a smile softening his face.

Suddenly he turned toward Deanna. She was glad for the masking glasses.

"I think I'll take the inner tube and join Mickey," he said. "How about you?"

"Not just now. In a bit, maybe."

Lee reached for the inner tube, then stopped. "Maybe I should use some sunscreen, too. I haven't had much sun this year. Can I use yours?"

Deanna handed him the bottle. "Help yourself." She watched him smooth the cream over his chest and shoulders.

"Do my back for me?" he asked, holding out the bottle.

"Uh, sure." She took the sunscreen from him and he knelt, facing the water.

Deanna squeezed some of the lotion onto her hands. Tentatively she touched her fingertips to his shoulders, then, steeling herself, rubbed her palms over his back briskly. Still, the feel of his skin, smooth beneath her hands, caused almost forgotten sensations to churn deep within her. It took all her strength to keep from splaying her fingers across his back, from caressing the heated satin beneath her palms. She bit her bottom lip nervously.

"There," she said after a moment, striving for nonchalance. "Nicely basted."

She was feeling more than just a little breathless and prayed it didn't show.

Lee stood up and turned to her with a lazy smile. "Magic fingers," he murmured, looking at her through half-closed eyes. "Let me know if you want me to reciprocate." He flexed his hands in her direction. "I'll be more than happy to oblige." Chuckling at the look on her face, he picked up a patched inner tube and strode down to the water.

Deanna watched his easy walk, her hands still tingling from the feel of his skin, and wondered just how it would feel to have him return the favor. Sighing, she rubbed her palms together, wondering at herself.

It was inevitable, she supposed. No matter how much she had loved Ryan and grieved his passing, sooner or later she was bound to feel something for another man, if only this niggling physical reaction. Still, it didn't rest comfortably with her. With Ryan, the attraction had been part of her love. With Lee... She sighed again and shook her head. She didn't know what to think.

He had changed since his return from California. Whether it was the shock of finding Wade Wescott in his home or the relief from business pressures or both, he was suddenly approachable. She liked the turnaround, the way he had opened up to her and the relationship he was beginning to establish with Mickey. She liked him, and that was fine. It was this growing awareness, these undeniable physical feelings, that disturbed her.

If it had been one-sided it wouldn't bother her so much. But it wasn't. Lee was feeling something, too. She saw it in his eyes, heard it in his teasing voice.

She wondered what she would do if he acted on his feelings. She felt a surge of excitement at the thought and groaned inwardly. This was not what she wanted, not at all.

Determined to put all such thoughts from her mind, Deanna pushed at the glasses sliding down her nose and looked out over the lake. Lee was lying back in the inner tube, arms and legs dangling, while Mickey tugged it along by a piece of nylon rope. She stopped and took a deep breath before disappearing beneath the surface. Coming up suddenly, she tipped the tube over, sending Lee into the water.

Grinning, Deanna watched Lee retaliate, sending a spray of water into Mickey's laughing face. As she squealed in protest, he took her by the arms and swung her around and around, her feet skimming the top of the water. When he released her, she sank briefly, then surfaced, sputtering with laughter. Flinging herself onto the inner tube, she pleaded for a ride.

Deanna was tempted to join in, but decided it was best to let them enjoy some time by themselves. And she was quite comfortable where she was. It felt wonderful to be out of the city, to have a chance to enjoy the prairie summer without the background hum of traffic and faint metallic smell of car exhaust in the heated air. Summers were made for lying on white sand beaches under azure skies.

After a few minutes, Deanna took a notebook and pen from her bag. She'd had little time for writing since she started looking after Mickey, and ideas for her book were pinging through her mind. Words came quickly, and she scribbled furiously, trying to keep pace.

"What are you writing?"

Blinking, Deanna looked up. Lee stood in front of her, water beading on his skin. He sluiced a hand over his face then shook his hair. Drops flew, some landing on her.

He grinned. "Sorry. On second thought, no, I'm not." He leaned closer, shaking his head again. "One way or another, you'll get wet today."

Deanna picked up a handful of sand and threatened to throw it. "And you'll get covered with sand if you don't back off."

His eyebrows rose over laughing eyes. "Oh, yeah?"

Deanna had to look away to hide the sudden rush of excitement, hoping he hadn't seen it. "Well, maybe not," she said lightly, letting the sand slide through her fingers. "You'd probably throw me in with the fish to get even."

"Good guess," he said, nodding.

She glanced up at him from over the top of her sunglasses. "Quit hovering and sit down," she said.

"Yes, ma'am," he said smartly, and obeyed. Taking a towel, he wiped his face and neck dry. "That felt good. It's been years since I've been to the lake."

The space under the umbrella seemed small suddenly, even confined. Surreptitiously, Deanna inched closer to the edge of the shade. "Mickey seemed to enjoy playing with you," she said.

Lee laughed. "She's a spunky little thing, isn't she? Not nearly as shy and quiet as I thought she was." He glanced at the notebook propped on her knees. "You didn't answer me. What are you writing?"

She shrugged and closed the book. "Just some ideas for the book I'm working on."

"Ah, yes. I saw Mickey engrossed with the one you gave her last night. She says it's 'neat.'"

"I'm glad she likes it."

"I glanced through it myself after she was asleep," he went on. "You've got quite an imagination. And..." He fell silent.

"And what?" she asked, wondering if he had some criticism to offer. She wouldn't like it, but she would listen.

"Well, it gave me some ideas," he said slowly. "For a computer game."

"Really?" Deanna knew little about computers and couldn't visualize it. "How do you mean?"

"Well, your heroine has all sorts of adventures—strange ones on bizarre worlds. And she has that pet that rides on her shoulder and throws webs..."

"Arachne the Spyther from Webworld," Deanna filled in a little self-consciously. She was beginning to think that he had done more than glance through her book.

Lee gave her a look. "As I said—bizarre," he murmured. "Anyway, I've got a hunch something could be made of it. I'd like to talk to my partner, Rick—he's the one behind the games. He's good, especially when he gets fired up about something."

The idea of someone coming up with a game based on her characters appealed to Deanna. "It sounds interesting," she said.

"Then you don't mind if I mention it to Rick? I'd like him to read the book and see what he can come up with."

"It's all right with me," Deanna said, shrugging.

"Good. You know, you write quite well. It might be a children's book, but I found your ideas and settings intriguing."

"Thank you," Deanna murmured, feeling embarrassed. It felt odd to have an adult, Lee especially, comment on her writing.

She looked to where Mickey was busy adding to her pile of water-scoured pebbles. Mickey glanced up, grinned and waved, then came running toward them.

"This is a neat place," she said, dropping to the sand. She scooped some up and let it trickle through her fingers. "Can we go for a walk down there?" She pointed to the far curve of beach.

"I wouldn't mind," Lee said. "Deanna?"

"What about our things?"

"I'll take the binoculars. The rest should be okay."

Mickey stood up, brushing sand from the bottom of her damp bathing suit. "Let's go!"

Deanna reached for her loose white cotton shirt and slipped it on over her bathing suit to keep the sun off her back and shoulders. She put a floppy-brim straw hat on her head and pushed at the sunglasses sliding down her nose. "I'm ready," she said, standing.

Lee got to his feet, his eyes sparking with laughter as he looked at her. "You sure you have enough clothes on?"

She made a face. "I burn," she said. "Then I freckle."

"No kidding," he drawled, his gaze traveling slowly up and down the long length of her legs. "I was thinking that if I got bored lying on the beach, I could play connect the dots."

Mickey looked at both of them, then burst into giggles. "That's funny, Uncle Lee."

"No, it's not," Deanna muttered, but her stomach had given a little leap at the glimmer she saw in his eyes. "Are we going on that walk or not?"

"We're going!" Mickey said, and dashed off ahead of them.

"She's in high spirits," Lee said as they followed along the water's edge.

"She's feeling better all round," Deanna said, glad to have Mickey the topic of conversation. It helped her keep errant thoughts under control. "Your spending time with her has made a real difference. She's beginning to feel like she belongs." She hesitated a moment, then asked, "Have you heard from her father?"

"Nothing. Not even a phone call to see if she's all right."

"Do you think he's gone?"

Lee shook his head. "Not this easily. He's probably been partying. He'll show up again."

"What are you going to do?"

"Take it one step at a time. I want to see his cards before I play mine."

"Just make sure you win," Deanna murmured, watching Mickey skip through the wavelets rippling onto shore.

"I will, Deanna," he said with quiet conviction. "He ruined Teri's life. I won't let him ruin her daughter's."

DEANNA WAS GLAD Lee seemed in no hurry to return to the city. As afternoon slipped into evening, the air became soft, filled with the fragrance of summer grasses. Terns flew parallel to the shore watching for silvery flashes of leaping minnows. Gulls trod the sand in bobbing stride, searching for scraps of food. The sun hovered over the water, moving slowly toward the horizon, and the lake was calm and mirror smooth. Mickey sat by its edge, molding damp sand into castle turrets.

Lee turned to Deanna. "Tell me about your husband," he said quietly.

Startled, Deanna looked up from the magazine she was reading and stared at him.

"I heard Mickey say something about him being sick like her mother," he said. "She mentioned it again yesterday. But if you don't want to talk about it..."

"No. No, it's not that. You took me by surprise, that's all." She laid the magazine down and sat forward, resting her chin on her knees, staring out over the water. "He had leukemia," she said finally. "He was sick for months." Nothing in her voice told of the agony she had gone through, her terrible sense of helplessness.

"Has it been long since he died?"

"Just over three years."

"You still miss him."

Frowning, Deanna poked at the sand. "Yes, I do. I miss sharing my life with him. Like when I sold my first book. He was the only one who would have understood how much it meant to me. We were good friends," she said softly, staring off into the distance. "I still feel lonely sometimes. It might be different if we'd had a chance to have the baby we wanted. At least I'd still have a part of him, but—"

She stopped suddenly, appalled to have said so much. Lee wanted a few facts about her life, not a melancholy tale. "Sorry," she murmured, embarrassed.

"Don't be." He sat silently, tossing a pebble from hand to hand.

Deanna glanced at him, seeing a different expression on his face. She had seen it before on other men when they'd learned she was a widow. The situation seemed to take them aback, made them treat her more gently. The flirting almost invariably stopped. Maybe it was just as well she had shared some of her pain with Lee. Maybe this way they could be friends.

"What about your family?" he asked after a moment. "Are they in Winnipeg?"

"Toronto," she said, glad he didn't ask more about Ryan. "My parents are both lawyers—retired, actually. My younger brother is a lawyer, too, and my sister is a doctor."

"How did you end up here?"

"I came out to stay with my aunt. I'm more like her than I am the rest of my family." Aunt Alice had saved her sanity after Ryan's death.

Deanna grinned suddenly and glanced at Lee. "'Ditzy' is the word my father likes to use. We decided if that meant we wouldn't make good lawyers, then we were quite happy to be ditzy."

Lee chuckled. "I can just imagine what it would be like having two of you next door."

"A regular little coven," Deanna murmured.

He laughed outright. "It crossed my mind," he admitted. The teasing glint was back in his eyes. "I can almost hear the midnight chants under a full moon accompanied by cats yowling on the wall."

Deanna shook her head reprovingly, but couldn't hide her smile. She enjoyed this lighthearted side of Lee. A lot. It was obvious by now that it was more his nature than the remote arrogance he'd displayed at first.

Mickey looked up and waved. "Come see!" she called. "It's finished."

Deanna acknowledged her with a raised hand and stood up, stretching a bit. "You, too," she said to Lee. "It's time to ooh and aah over your niece's creativity."

Lee extended a lazy hand. "Help me up."

With a reluctance that surprised her, Deanna took his hand. His lean fingers curled around hers and tightened. She gave a little tug.

"Harder," he murmured, watching her through narrowed eyes.

Deanna wrapped both her hands around his and planted her feet firmly in the ground. She tugged again.

Lee jumped to his feet, throwing her off balance. She landed on her rear in the sand.

"Oof," she muttered, glaring at him. "Just see if I lend you a hand again."

Grinning, he extended his. "Help you up?"

"Forget it." She got to her feet and brushed the sand from the back of her legs with a nonchalance that wasn't as real as she would have liked. She was very aware that Lee followed the movements of her hands closely.

"I'm getting bored," he murmured, a glint in his eyes. "Got a pen I can use?"

"Behave yourself," Deanna reproved.

"Or what?" he challenged.

"I'll turn you into a toad."

"Make it a frog. Then you can kiss me and turn me back into Prince Charming."

Just the thought of kissing him made her heart beat a little faster. "News flash, Mr. Stratton," she said coolly. "You are not Prince Charming."

"No? What am I then?"

Deanna put her head to one side and tapped a finger against her chin, looking at him thoughtfully. "I haven't quite decided yet."

Mickey looked up from her sand castle and called out impatiently, "Come on, you guys!"

Lee grinned at Deanna and closed one eye in a wink as he turned and walked toward Mickey.

Deanna followed slowly, amazed by how much Lee's appeal had grown in the past few hours.

They examined and dutifully admired the castle to Mickey's obvious pleasure.

"Maybe you can be an engineer when you grow up," Lee said.

Mickey looked up doubtfully. "You mean drive a train?"

Laughing, Lee shook his head. "I mean someone who designs roads and bridges, things like that. That's an engineer, too."

"Naw. I wouldn't want to do that. I'm going to write books, like Deanna. Or be an astronaut." She poked a broken edge of a freshwater clam shell into the turret of the castle. "It would be neat to be in space."

"Sounds good to me," Deanna said. She looked out over the lake. The sky paled as the sun sank toward the horizon, shooting a rippling trail of light across the water. "It's getting late," she said. "Why don't we go for a walk before we have to head home?"

"Sure," Lee said easily. "I'm in no hurry to get back. Mickey?"

"Okay." The girl stood up, took a few steps backward and then ran toward the sand castle. Leaping into the air, she landed on it with both feet and a yell. Grinning, she turned to face the adults. "There's no point in letting someone else wreck it, is there?" She reached out and took each of them by the hand. "Let's go."

Night was fast approaching by the time they returned to pack up their things. The sun had dropped just below the horizon, and the thin, stretching clouds to the west cast their molten glow over the water. A star poked through the sky where paler blue deepened to indigo. The birds had made their last flights of the day. The air was still and quiet.

Mickey pulled a sweatshirt on over her bathing suit while Deanna and Lee packed up. She stood with her arms held tight to her chest, staring up at the star. Her shoulders hunched a little and she began murmuring.

Deanna could hear enough to know she was making a wish. She glanced up herself, the lines running through her mind. *Star light, star bright, first star I see tonight...*

She sighed softly and looked away. She had a wish, too, one she didn't dare allow her mind to embrace....

CHAPTER SEVEN

THE CITY LIGHTS obscured the stars as the three of them drove into Winnipeg. The car radio played softly while Mickey slept in the back. Deanna sat beside Lee, comfortable with his silence.

It had been a very good day, all in all. The only thing that bothered Deanna was her unwilling attraction to Lee. It had grown by leaps and bounds, had become more than mere attraction. She'd enjoyed herself with him today. She'd liked his gentle teasing, the flash of green light in his eyes when he laughed.

They were well on their way to becoming friends, but a little voice told her they could be more. What would she do if he made a move?

Lee slowed and stopped for a red light. He turned to take a quick look at Mickey. "She's exhausted," he said. "We didn't overdo it, did we? It's only been a couple of days since she was sick."

Deanna smiled a little at the worry coloring his voice. It was good to hear. "She's all right. Just tired out. She had a great time today. It did her more good than harm."

"It was fun, wasn't it?" he said, accelerating the engine as the light turned green. He changed gears, then lanes, his driving fast but careful.

Deanna let the silence fall between them again, but any sense of relaxation she'd had was gone. She was too conscious of Lee sitting beside her. She watched covertly as the passing lights illuminated his face. His eyes darted back and forth as he watched the traffic. He steered with one hand, the other resting on the stick shift.

She was aware of every movement of his arm as he changed gears. It didn't quite brush against hers, but her skin still tingled. Pulling closer to the door, she rubbed a hand up and down her upper arm.

"Cold?" he asked with a quick glance at her.

"Not at all," she answered.

"Well, anyway, we're almost home."

"Good. I can't wait to shower off all this sand and sun-screen."

"A shower would feel pretty good right about now," Lee agreed. He downshifted and changed lanes to make a left-hand turn. "I feel like I've got half the beach sticking to my back."

Deanna leaned against the headrest, remembering the warm satiny feel of his skin beneath her fingers as she'd rubbed the sunscreen over his shoulders. Tiredly she closed her eyes and tried to push the memory away....

It was after eleven by the time they parked behind Lee's house. Mickey was sound asleep. Lee picked her up and carried her while Deanna went on ahead.

She pulled the covers on Mickey's bed back, then stood aside while Lee carefully laid her down. Mickey frowned and murmured incoherently.

"She shouldn't sleep in her bathing suit," Deanna said, speaking softly. "Could you get her a nightgown from the middle drawer while I undress her?" She sat on the edge of the bed and lifted Mickey to take off her sweatshirt and bathing suit.

"I'm tired," Mickey protested, her eyes still closed.

"I know, sweetheart. This'll just take a minute. You'll be more comfortable in your nightie. Arms up now—that's a girl." She took the nightgown from Lee and dropped it over Mickey's head. With a whimper of protest, Mickey fumbled her arms into the sleeves, then dropped onto the pillow. Smiling, Deanna straightened the nightgown, then pulled up the top sheet and blanket, smoothing them around Mickey's shoulders.

"Good night, sweetheart." She kissed her forehead. "See you tomorrow."

Lee briefly rested his hand on his niece's hair. "Night, Mickey," he said. "It was fun today."

Sighing, Mickey rolled over, tucking a hand under her cheek. She was asleep. Lee and Deanna left the room, closing the door quietly behind them.

"I enjoyed myself," Deanna said over her shoulder as she led the way down the hall to the kitchen. "Thank you."

"Thank you for coming," Lee returned. "You've made it easier for me with Mickey. I appreciate that."

"I'm just glad to see things working out," Deanna said. "Looks like you two are going to have a good relationship." She grinned suddenly. "Mickey thinks you're a much nicer person since you got back from California."

Lee's eyebrows rose. "Did she actually say that?"

"Uh-huh. She thinks something nice must have happened to you there." Deanna's clear gray eyes sparkled with laughter. "What was it?"

"I signed the deal of a lifetime."

"That's it? Nothing personal?" Under the teasing banter, she really wanted to know. She thought of the woman who'd answered the phone in his hotel room.

Lee gave a short laugh. "I don't have a personal life. Until Mickey came along, it's been nothing but business."

What was it going to be now? Deanna wondered, but said nothing. She glanced at the clock on the stove.

"I should be getting home," she said. "I'll just collect the rest of my things from the car."

"Leave them until tomorrow," Lee said dismissively. "Listen . . . I was thinking of relaxing with a drink. Would you like to join me?"

Deanna hesitated, a little surprised at the invitation.

"Just one," he coaxed. "Gin and tonic?"

"Um . . . all right. I guess the shower can wait."

"Good. Why don't you go sit by the pool while I mix them?"

"All right. But make mine with lots of tonic and ice, please. I don't drink much."

Lee set two tall glasses on the counter. "Okay. Do you want anything to eat?"

"What have you got?"

"I think there's a can of cashews in the cupboard. How's that?"

"Perfect," Deanna said. She pushed open the door and went onto the deck. As she took a seat, the pool lights came on, filtering up through the water. It looked inviting.

Deanna stood and shrugged off the shirt and shorts she had pulled on over her bathing suit. Walking to the edge of the pool, she slid into the water. It felt cold for a moment, then silkily refreshing. She dove under, then surfacing, swam to the deep end and back again. She hauled herself out and sat on the edge. Tilting her head to one side, she wrung the water from her hair.

Lee came out carrying the drinks and a couple of towels draped over his arm. He set the drinks on the patio table.

"I thought you might be tempted," he said, dropping a towel over her shoulders.

"Thank you," she murmured. She took a corner of the towel and wiped her face dry.

Lee walked around the pool and onto the diving board. He stood for a moment, bouncing lightly up and down.

Deanna watched, appreciating the lithe lines of his body as he executed a clean dive. Sighing a little, she got up and went to sit by the table.

She picked up her drink and took a sip. The cool, tart liquid was welcome. She took another swallow, then settled back in her chair, cradling the glass in her hands as she stared moodily at Lee stroking sleekly through the water. She'd felt the pull of attraction even when she hadn't really liked him. But now...

A physical reaction was one thing. She was young and healthy, and Lee was undeniably attractive. But she was beginning to feel more than that for him, and it disturbed her. She didn't want to fall for him, to leave herself vulnerable and open to pain. She took another drink, a frown settling on her face.

Lee climbed out of the pool, water running from his body. He picked up a towel and wiped his face. "That felt great," he said. Draping the towel across his shoulders, he sat down opposite Deanna. As he reached for his drink, he caught sight of her face.

"Deanna? Is something wrong?"

"No, nothing," she assured him hastily. "I'm just tired, that's all. I should be going." She put down her glass and got to her feet. "It's been a long day."

Lee got up, as well. "I'll walk you home," he said. "Unless you'd rather climb the fence?"

Deanna forced a little laugh as she gathered her clothes and beach bag. "Not tonight," she said. She kept the towel wrapped around her shoulders as she thrust her feet into her sandals. "You don't have to come with me."

"But I will. Got your key?"

Deanna fished in her bag and hooked the key ring around her finger. She would rather he stayed, but she wasn't going to argue with him. "Right here," she said, jangling them. "I'll get the rest of my things tomorrow."

They walked quietly through the house and out the front door. The night was quiet but for the sporadic hum of distant traffic, the air soft with lingering heat. Deanna fumbled with her key in the lock and opened the door.

She turned to Lee, pulling the towel a little tighter around her shoulders. "It was a lovely day," she said formally. "Thank you."

He stood in front of her, his face shadowed. Streetlight filtered through the trees on the boulevard and touched his skin. Casually he reached out and tucked a wet lock of her hair behind her ear. "Yes, it was," he said. "You're fun to be with." A smile played on his face as he bent closer. His mouth brushed hers.

Deanna exhaled sharply, her breath mingling with his. She could feel the damp heat of his body soak into her skin, though he touched her with nothing save his caressing mouth. Her lips clung as little sparks of pleasure coursed through her.

She pulled back suddenly, her eyes wide with conflicting emotions. "Don't," she whispered. "Please don't. I'm not..." She shook her head in confusion. "I just can't." Biting her lip, she shook her head again, then fled inside.

She shut the door and stood there in the dark hallway, tears pricking her eyes.

He was the first man to kiss her since Ryan. It wouldn't have been so bad if she'd felt nothing. But his kiss, undemanding as it was, left her with mixed feelings of desire and disloyalty.

She'd known she was attracted to him, but the intensity of the feelings aroused by his lips on hers had taken her completely by surprise. It was far too much, too soon.

SHE SPENT a restless night and was awake much earlier than she would normally have been. Taking a cup of coffee out into the backyard, she sat with the cats, watching the robins feed the fledglings that filled the nest to overflowing with their plump, speckle-breasted bodies.

She brooded over her reactions to Lee. It had been just a simple kiss. Why couldn't she have accepted it as such, given a little laugh and an amusing comment to lighten the moment? Now it would hang over them, giving the kiss more meaning than it actually had.

She heard the back gate open and looked up sharply. Lee was there, coming toward her. She put her coffee cup down on the lawn and nervously smoothed her palms over her skirt. "Good morning," she said as easily as she could.

He nodded abruptly, his hair falling softly against his forehead. He took the seat beside her. "Can I talk to you?"

Not about last night, she pleaded silently.

"I want to apologize."

Deanna shook her head quickly. "It's okay. I know I overreacted. It's just..." She stopped and looked down, shrugging in embarrassment.

"You haven't been with anyone since your husband died," Lee supplied. "Am I right?"

She didn't raise her eyes. "Yes."

"You loved him very much."

Deanna lifted her head and looked at him with a vulnerability she couldn't hide. "Yes."

He watched her through narrowed eyes, then gently touched a finger to her cheek. "I'm sorry," he said softly, and Deanna knew he was referring to more than their brief kiss last night. She smiled with difficulty and nodded.

Leaning forward suddenly, he rested his arms on his knees. "I need to talk to you about something else—about Mickey."

"Where is she?" Deanna asked, glad for a change of subject.

"Still asleep. I taped a note to her door telling her I was over here. I wanted to talk to you before she was up."

"All right. Why don't we go into the house? I've got coffee on."

Lee followed Deanna into the kitchen and waited while she took a mug from the cupboard.

"Just black," he said as she poured.

She handed him the mug and leaned against the counter watching him. He was more understanding—and insightful—than she'd thought he might be. A lot of men would have been put off. Lee had accepted her feelings. She felt a warm little glow that grew as she waited for him to speak.

Lee pulled out a chair and sat down at the table. "There was a message on the answering machine this morning," he said. "Wescott wants Mickey for the day."

"Oh, no." Deanna felt some of his apprehension. She'd hoped Mickey's father had faded from the picture. "What are you going to do?"

"I know what I *want* to do," he said with an angry scowl. "But I don't know what I *should* do. For Mickey's sake."

Deanna was glad he hadn't given in to his first impulse. Pouring herself a fresh cup of coffee, she went to sit across from Lee.

"I wondered what you thought," he continued.

"Have you talked to a lawyer about this?"

"Of course." He raked his fingers through his hair. "She says that keeping Mickey from visiting her father will look bad should this thing ever go to court. I've got to show I was willing to let Mickey develop a relationship with him."

"In the long run, then, you don't have a lot of choice."

"I suppose not. But what if he decides to keep her?"

"Do you really think he will?"

Lee sighed and shook his head. "He doesn't really want Mickey, I'm sure of that, but he'll want to make things difficult for me."

"I think the lawyer's right. You can't not let her see him," Deanna said. "He is her father, after all."

"He gave up his parental rights a long time ago."

"But not in Mickey's eyes. She's not going to see him the way we do. Not at this point in her life. I think she should be given the chance to get to know him. And I've got a hunch that when she does, she won't want to spend much time with him."

Still scowling, Lee rubbed the back of his neck. "Not if she's half as smart as I think she is. I still don't like it, though. I don't trust him."

"You're probably right not to." She ran a finger around the rim of her mug, staring down thoughtfully. "You're going to have to make sure you know exactly where he's taking her—and get the address of the place where he's staying." She looked up. "I don't think he really wants her, either. He's probably doing this as much to get at you as anything. So don't let him see that it bothers you. Just smile and say, 'Have a nice day.' "

Lee made an expression of disgust and she had to laugh. "Maybe you should practice a bit," she said, her eyes sparkling. "You wouldn't fool him for an instant with that look on your face."

He curled his lips in a snarling smile. "How's this?" he asked through his teeth.

"Stop! You're scaring me."

There was a sudden rap on the front door and they heard it open.

"It's me!" Mickey's voice preceded her down the hall. She stood in the doorway to the kitchen and grinned. "I saw your note, Uncle Lee. I came right over."

"I can see that," Lee said, raising his eyebrows at his niece. She was dressed in clean shorts and a T-shirt, but she hadn't stopped to brush her hair. It was still tangled and sticking up in back.

Mickey stood there staring at them, a thoughtful look on her face.

"Did you stay here last night, Uncle Lee?" she asked, her pale blue eyes round with curiosity.

Lee sputtered on a mouthful of coffee. Swallowing hastily, he wiped the back of a hand across his mouth.

"Well, did you?" she demanded.

"Of course he didn't," Deanna answered for him, her eyes alight with laughter.

"Oh." Disappointment flashed across Mickey's face.

"Your uncle and I are just friends, sweetie," Deanna said. "Only people who are in love spend the night together."

Mickey sighed. "Yeah, I s'pose. Are the cats outside?" she asked.

"All three. You can go play with them if you want."

"Okay." Mickey went to the back door and opened it. "I didn't have breakfast yet," she said.

"Then I'll make something for all of us," Deanna assured her. "I'll call you when it's ready."

"Okay," Mickey said again. She went outside, calling to the cats.

"Where in the world did she come up with *that?*" Lee asked as the door closed behind her.

Deanna looked away from him, remembering his kiss and the way it had made her feel. It would have been so easy to let him . . . She stopped that thought, but not before a picture of them together flashed through her mind.

With Mickey out of the room, the humor of the situation lessened. She tried to fight her discomfort and speak calmly.

"Kids today know a lot more than we ever did," she explained, getting up to pour more coffee.

"Maybe Teri had . . . friends."

"Not necessarily," Deanna said. "She probably picked it up from TV. And from other kids. It's no big deal." But she could see the direction Mickey's thoughts were heading. She hoped her expectations wouldn't get out of hand.

"So, would you like some breakfast?" she asked.

"If it isn't too much trouble."

"No trouble at all. I'm starving. How does a ham-and-cheese omelet sound?"

"Great," Lee said. "Can I help?"

"No, thanks. I can manage. Why don't you go outside and talk to Mickey about her father?"

Lee grimaced. "I suppose I should."

"And Lee, keep your feelings out of it," Deanna advised quietly. "Think of her."

"I am," Lee said grimly as he got up. "That's what makes me want to get rid of Wescott once and for all."

THE PHONE RANG shortly after eight that evening. Deanna put down her pen and got up, smiling as the budgies made their usual raucous response to the jangling tones.

The caller was Lee. "Deanna? Would you mind coming over, please?"

Something in his voice stopped her from asking questions. "I'll be right there." She hung up, grabbed her purse and left.

Lee was standing on his front steps. He looked hot. His linen pants and cotton shirt were creased, and his hair had fallen over his forehead.

"He hasn't brought Mickey back yet," he said as she approached.

"Oh, no," Deanna said. "What time did you tell him to have her here?"

"I told him eight o'clock at the latest." He glanced at his watch. "I know it's not much past that, but I phoned the number he gave me to remind him. He's not there, Deanna," he said grimly. "They told me they'd asked him to leave yesterday. As far as they know, he got a room in this area, but they don't know where—and don't much care, I gathered."

He raked his fingers through his hair and paced restlessly. "Damn it, Deanna. I should have gone with my instincts, not some damned lawyer's advice!!"

"Lee, you couldn't have known—"

"Yes, I could have. I should never have let her go. How am I supposed to find her? There are dozens of rooms and cheap apartments for rent in the city."

"I'm sure he'll bring her back soon, Lee," Deanna said, but her own concern was growing rapidly. "He'll probably keep her out a little late just to try and get to you."

"I hope you're right. But in the meantime, would you mind using your phone to call some of the rooming houses listed in the phone book? I'd use mine, but I want the line open in case Mickey calls."

"I'll get started right away," she said, turning to go down the steps. "And, Lee, it'll be all right. I'm sure."

"I wish I was," he said, his voice tight and cold.

DEANNA MADE HER CALLS and came up with nothing. Wade Wescott was not to be found. Her stomach knotted in worry, she hurried back to Lee's.

He was pacing the small porch, but stopped when he saw her coming.

"No luck," she said. "Sorry."

He leaned tiredly against the side of the house, looking off down the street. "I want her back."

Deanna heard both frustration and guilt in his voice. "So do I." She laid a sympathetic hand on his arm. "Would you like a cold drink?" she asked.

"Please. Thank you," he added absently.

"What would you like?"

"Anything long and icy will do."

"Okay. I'll be right back."

She went into his kitchen and poured orange juice into tall glasses, added ice cubes and a splash of soda water. She

hoped Mickey was okay, that Wade was simply late bringing her back. Anything else was intolerable, for her as much
as for Lee. She wanted the girl home, safe and sound, where
she belonged.

Deanna carried the drinks outside. Lee was sitting on the
top step, his face deeply etched with worry. She handed him
a glass and sat down.

Her old gray tom had followed her over and was approaching cautiously. He stayed on a lower step but leaned
tautly forward to sniff at Lee's foot. Then, with a flick of his
tail, Leo turned and stalked away, ears laid back.

"He still doesn't like you," Deanna said, in an attempt to
distract Lee. "Maybe he just resents your name—it's too
much like his. Of course he doesn't like most people. I'm
okay because I feed him—and Mickey, too, naturally. All
the cats adore her."

Lee took a swallow of his drink. "This is perfect. Thank
you. I was thinking of getting Mickey a kitten," he added.

"How about Alfie and Imp?" Deanna suggested impulsively. "She loves them. And they're already housebroken,
neutered and have had all their shots."

"Are you trying to get rid of them?" He kept staring
down the street. He was saying the words, but his mind was
elsewhere.

"Not really, but I only took them in because no one else
would. My aunt will be putting this place up for sale before
much longer. It'll be hard for me to find somewhere that'll
let me have one cat, never mind three. If it's all right with
you, I'd like to give them to Mickey for her birthday next
month."

"If you're sure, I don't see why not. She'd be delighted." He took another sip, then glanced around the yard.
"So your aunt is going to sell."

"That's her plan. She wanted to try a year in Victoria first
to see if she liked it—and apparently she loves it. She'll

probably put the house on the market this fall. I imagine it'll go fast."

"In this area, probably. You aren't considering buying it yourself?"

Deanna laughed and shook her head. "There's no way I'd be able to afford it."

"So what will you do?"

"I really don't know. I might decide to move out to Victoria myself. I'll see what I feel like doing when the time comes." She poked absently at an ice cube floating in her drink. Just a little while ago the thought of moving, with the whole of Canada to pick from, had been immensely appealing. Lately she felt as though she'd be quite happy to stay where she was. She glanced at Lee and knew with a sudden flash of insight that moving away from here—from him—was the last thing she wanted to do.

"Mickey will miss you."

"And I'll miss her." *What about you?* she wanted to ask. Would Lee miss her as much as she knew she'd miss him? "But she'll be in school then, making all kinds of new friends. And she'll have you."

Lee scowled and glanced at his watch. "If Wescott doesn't screw things up, that is. Damn it. I can't stand waiting around, doing nothing." He jumped to his feet and began to prowl the length of the porch, frustrated by circumstances that wouldn't let him take control.

"He'll bring her back, Lee," Deanna said, more worried than she let on.

"Will he?" Lee stopped his pacing abruptly and turned to her. "What if he's decided to keep Mickey? He could be halfway to Saskatchewan by now—or anywhere else for that matter. I've got to call the police. I took down his license— the RCMP can start looking for his car."

"Hang on, Lee," Deanna said quickly. "It's too soon for that. You don't know that he's taken her. Wait a bit. He's probably just keeping her out late to worry you. I'm sure he doesn't really want her. She'd just get in his way. Wait another hour, at least. She'll be back by then."

"I hope you're right," Lee muttered, rubbing the back of his neck.

"I am," Deanna said with more confidence than she felt.

Leo reappeared and trotted up to Deanna, tail held high as he bumped against her hand. She scratched absently between his ears, watching as Lee glanced yet again at his watch.

"Nine o'clock," he said tersely, and resumed his pacing.

Deanna could feel his tenseness. It coiled around him, ready to spring forth as anger. She hoped he'd be able to control himself for Mickey's sake. The child didn't need to see her father and her uncle going at it again.

"Lee," she said, "when they get here... I know you're angry, but try not to let it show. Don't make Mickey have to choose sides."

Lee stopped and stared at her, his eyes dark with suppressed fury.

"Don't worry," Deanna said gently. "I'm not asking you to smile nicely at the guy. Just give me a minute to take Mickey inside. Then you can let him have it!"

Surprisingly Lee chuckled. He sat back down beside her, leaning forward, his arms resting on his knees. "No violence," he said. "I promise."

"Good." She touched his arm lightly in comfort, then perked up as a car turned onto the street and drove their way. It went past without stopping. Deanna sighed, her shoulders sagging.

"You're just as worried as I am," Lee said, watching her.

This time Deanna admitted it. "I know. I just want her home where she belongs."

"So do—" Lee stopped abruptly and Deanna followed his gaze.

Mickey was coming down the street, backlit by the setting sun, her shadow stretching long and thin in front of her. When Lee called her name, she started running toward them.

Her face was grimy and streaked with tears. She paused for a moment just inside the yard, looking tired and utterly dejected.

"Mickey..." Deanna gazed worriedly at the girl.

With a cry, Mickey ran down the sidewalk and hurled herself at Deanna, wrapping her arms tight around her neck and burrowing her face into her shoulder.

"I want my mom!" she wailed. "I just want my mom!"

"Oh, sweetheart," Deanna murmured, holding her tight. "I know you do." She rocked back and forth, her eyes brimming. She looked at Lee.

His face was stony with anger. He opened his mouth to speak, but drew a deep, calming breath, instead. Reaching out, he laid a comforting hand on his niece's head.

"What happened, Mickey?" he asked. "Where's your father?"

Mickey raised her head slowly from Deanna's shoulder and sighed tremulously. "He...he's at his place," she said, wiping a hand across her eyes. Tears smeared on her face.

"What happened?" Lee asked again. Deanna could see her own fears reflected on his face. "What did you do today?"

"Nothin'." Mickey shook her head. "He and his friend just sat and drank beer all day. We didn't do nothin', not go to the zoo or anything. I just had to sit there while they played cards and acted real stupid." Her bottom lip pushed out.

Deanna stroked the hair back from Mickey's damp forehead. "That doesn't sound like it was much fun for you."

"It sure wasn't," Mickey agreed. "And when I said I wanted to come home, he got real mad and said I should shut up and he would take me back when he was good and ready and that might be never."

Lee's narrowed eyes met Deanna's. He asked the question that was on both their minds.

"Mickey, did your father . . . hurt you?"

Mickey shook her head. "No. He just got mad sometimes. I didn't like it." She twisted around in Deanna's arms and kicked at the top step. "He's not very nice," she said despondently.

"Most people aren't when they've been drinking," Deanna said. She heard the broken dreams in Mickey's voice. Any illusions the girl had had about her father were shattered.

Lee ran a gentle finger over the curve of Mickey's face. He smiled when she turned to look at him, her pale blue eyes wide with emotion.

"Did you have to walk far?"

She shook her head again. "Just five blocks. I counted."

"Does he know you came back here?"

"I guess." She shrugged. "There was a pen on the table, so I wrote that I was going home, then snuck out when I went to the bathroom. I would have phoned you to come and get me," she added earnestly, "but there was no phone. And I knew I could find my way here."

"I'm glad you did, Mickey," Lee said. "I missed you."

The girl smiled a little shyly. "Me, too," she said, ducking her head. She cast him a sidelong look. "Do I have to go with him again?"

"No," Lee said firmly, his eyes darkening.

Deanna hoped he could keep that promise. She pulled Mickey back into her arms for another hug, happy to have her home safe and sound.

Mickey laid her head on Deanna's shoulder, rubbing one hand nervously against the other. "He said he could come and get me anytime,'' she said in a low voice. ''That he's my father and you're only my uncle.''

''Your mother wanted you to live with me,'' Lee said, taking Mickey's hands in his and stroking them comfortingly. ''I promised her you would. No one will take you if you don't want to go.''

''Good. I just want to stay with you and Deanna.''

Deanna felt her heart give a little twist. Sooner or later Mickey would have to accept that Deanna wasn't part of the home Lee had promised to give her.

''I don't want to have to leave,'' Mickey whispered, still in need of assurance.

''You won't have to,'' Lee said. He met Deanna's eyes and held them for a moment, his expression unreadable. ''I'll do whatever I have to to keep you with me, Mickey. You don't have to worry anymore.''

Deanna blinked and looked away, afraid of what he might see in her eyes.

She returned home shortly afterward, sitting outside long after dark.

It was impossible to deny the feelings that tonight had taken firm hold of her heart. She sighed and wearily rubbed her forehead. She thought of Ryan, but for the first time another man's face came to mind. She saw the green glints in Lee's laughing eyes, saw his warm smile, the lock of hair falling over his forehead . . .

Had she fallen in love with him?

CHAPTER EIGHT

"IF YOU'RE GOING OUT together, then it's like a date," Mickey said. She was sitting cross-legged on Deanna's bed, carefully dabbing polish onto her nails. The bottle balanced precariously on one knee.

Deanna turned from the mirror. "No, it's not a date," she said firmly. "Your uncle asked me out for supper. That's all. It's just a meal, Mickey. Nothing more."

She couldn't help but wish Mickey was right, that Lee was taking her out on a real date, not just so they could have some quiet time to talk about Mickey and her father.

Mickey spread her fingers and held up her hand, examining her nails. "But I'm not going."

Deanna grabbed the nail polish bottle before it could spill onto the bedspread. "Not tonight. We're going on a riverboat for the dinner-and-dance cruise—it's not really for children."

"Dancing, too?" Mickey grinned as she handed the brush to Deanna. "Sure sounds like a date to me."

Deanna gave up and turned back to the mirror. Mickey was determined to believe that Lee and Deanna were going out on a date. And Deanna was equally determined not to allow herself the same fantasy.

Lee had hardly been home over the past several days. He hadn't really spoken to her other than to say he was trying to straighten things out with Mickey's father once and for all. He'd been talking to his lawyer and had met with Wade

Wescott more than once. Deanna assumed Lee would let her know the outcome of those meetings tonight.

Mickey spread her hands flat on the bed, admiring the deep pink polish. "If Uncle Lee gets married, then his wife will be my aunt, right?"

"That's right," Deanna answered absently, thinking ahead to tonight. What would it be like sharing an evening with Lee without Mickey? Dining and dancing, being held in his arms while the music swelled around them . . .

"And their babies would be my cousins, right? Only, almost like brothers and sisters, because Uncle Lee is kinda more than my uncle, 'cause I live with him."

Deanna had to smile. "Don't get your hopes up, kiddo," she said lightly. "As far as I know, your uncle doesn't even have a girlfriend."

That was a good thought. As long as there was no other woman in the picture, there was room for her.

"It could be just you and him for a long time yet," Deanna cautioned.

"And you," Mickey said confidently. She squirmed around on the bed until she was on her stomach, propping her chin on her hands.

"But I might not always be here," Deanna told her, wishing she could say otherwise. "When my aunt sells this house, I'll have to move—and I don't know where that'll be."

"Well, I think you should move in with us."

"Oh, you do, do you? And what happens when your uncle brings home that aunt you want?" They both had to be prepared for that. There were no guarantees that Lee wouldn't meet someone and fall in love.

"But I think it should be you." Mickey glanced at the picture of Ryan on the bedside table. "Your husband wouldn't mind if you got married again, would he?"

The question took Deanna completely by surprise. She looked at Ryan's face, forever unresponsive behind the protective glass. "I don't suppose he would," she said softly. Ryan had said as much before he died, urging her to go on with her life. And she had—except for personal involvement with a man.

"So you could marry Uncle Lee!" Behind her teasing grin, Mickey was serious.

That didn't really surprise Deanna. Mickey's world had been completely turned around over the past couple of months. Of course she'd want the two adults she had become fond of to stay together, caring for her.

Deanna smiled and shook her head. "Thanks for the idea, but no. Only people in love get married. Your uncle and I are just friends." And that was all. Lee had given no signs that he felt otherwise, in spite of what she was beginning to feel for him. There was some attraction on his part, yes. But love? Definitely not.

Mickey sighed. "Just thought I'd try," she muttered.

Feeling more than a little wishful herself, Deanna glanced at the clock. Lee would be back with the baby-sitter from the agency soon. It was time for her to finish getting dressed and take Mickey next door.

She slipped into a sundress with thin shoulder straps and close fitting bodice above a swirling skirt. It was black with a subtle pattern of color around the hem, and had a matching shawl for later, should the night turn cool.

She wore more makeup than usual, carefully emphasizing her clear gray eyes. Her hair gleamed with red and gold highlights, curling in studied disarray and sweeping her bare shoulders with every movement of her head.

"You look real pretty," Mickey said. "I'll bet Uncle Lee'll think so, too."

"Thank you," Deanna smiled fondly at the girl. She wanted Lee to notice her, to see her in a different light.

Maybe then that bit of attraction he felt for her would begin to grow.

DINNER WAS RELAXING. They ate to the sounds of a calypso band while the banks of the Red River slipped by.

"I've been on the paddle-wheel boats before," Deanna informed Lee. "But this is my first time at night. This was a great idea. Thanks."

Lee sat back in his chair, cradling a snifter of cognac in his hands. His smile didn't quite reach his eyes. He raised his glass to his lips and took a sip.

"It's been a long week," he said.

Deanna's patience was wearing thin. She needed to know how things had gone with Mickey's father. "Tell me about it," she said, resting her elbows on the table as she leaned closer.

"I paid him off."

Deanna's eyes widened. "What?"

Lee took another swallow of cognac. "I gave him exactly what he wanted. Ten thousand dollars bought his promise to leave Mickey alone." He shook his head in contempt. "The man's scum, Deanna. It's what he was angling for the whole time. He doesn't give a damn about Mickey."

"I've come to realize that," Deanna murmured. She was frowning. The whole situation left her with a bad feeling. "Do you trust him?" she asked. "I mean, won't he be around again for more? I doubt the money will last long."

"I told him this was it. And I had him write a letter saying that as far as he was concerned I was Mickey's legal guardian and that he was giving up any claim to her. It's all in his own handwriting, including the fact that he asked for payment. I wasn't going to have him say that I coerced him into signing anything."

He gave a short, contemptuous laugh. "You should have seen him, Deanna. He'd have done anything to get his hands on that check. It was ugly."

She found it all too easy to visualize the avarice on Wescott's face. Deanna only hoped Mickey would never find out what her father had done.

"But he will try again, won't he, Lee?" she said softly.

He sighed. "Yes, he probably will. He'll want more money. But I'm telling you he won't get any. I don't care what he threatens to do."

"Did you talk to your lawyer?"

"After the fact. Wescott's letter isn't binding of course, but it will make him look bad should he go for legal custody."

"Do you think he'll still try?"

"He'll be back when the party's over," Lee said with grim certainty. "If I don't give him more money, he probably will take it to court."

"He'll never get her, will he, Lee? No one could give her to him, not after what he's done."

"Nothing is ever positive, Deanna. I know I've got the better chance, but the fact still remains that he's her father. And who knows what kind of picture he'll manage to present? The man is a lazy, greedy bastard—but he isn't stupid."

"It's scary," Deanna said, rubbing her hands up and down her bare arms. She would hate to see Mickey in her father's custody.

"It is, isn't it?" He was looking at her closely, his eyes narrowing as he studied her face. "Deanna—" He stopped and shook his head as her brows rose in query. "Would you like another liqueur?"

"Not just now, thank you." That wasn't the question he'd been going to ask, she was sure. What had he really wanted to say?

"Then let's go outside," he said, pushing his chair back.

Deanna followed him out onto the deck and stood beside him, leaning against the railing to stare down at the brown-green water peeling back from the bow with a froth of white. A family of mallards bobbed in the wake, and from the shore, a great blue heron, neck crooked, took flight. The warm breeze caught and carried pockets of cooler air, rich with moist river scent, to brush against them. The sun was setting in the northwestern sky, shooting gold and red along the horizon.

She was very aware of Lee standing beside her and cast a covert glance his way. Lord, he was handsome, she thought, experiencing a surge of desire that still managed to take her by surprise. She hadn't reconciled herself completely to the fact that she was falling in love with him, even though her feelings for him grew with each passing day.

If it wasn't for Mickey, would they have any kind of relationship at all? she wondered. Was his niece the only reason he wanted her around, or did he have feelings for her that could stand on their own?

Deanna moved restlessly, sensing the warmth of Lee's arm where it rested next to hers on the railing.

Inside, the band began a new number, the calypso beat mingling with the muted throb of the ship's engines. Lee's hand came to rest on her arm.

Startled, she turned to look at him, her eyes wide as they met his.

"Deanna, I—" He shook his head again, a frown of impatience furrowing his brow. He took his hand from her arm, the tips of his fingers brushing her skin. "Do you want to dance?" he asked abruptly.

Again she was sure that wasn't what he'd been going to ask. "All right," she said calmly. "That would be lovely."

He gave her an odd little smile and reached for her hand. "Let's go."

She followed him inside and they joined the other dancers.

Deanna felt awkward. It'd been a long time since she'd danced, and much as she wanted to, it seemed strange to be doing so with Lee. He moved with an easy masculine grace, his touch light and impersonal as he stared off over her shoulder. When she glanced at his face, she could see the distance in his eyes. It was obvious he was just going through the motions. He didn't really want to dance.

"We don't have to do this," she offered.

"I'm sorry." He blinked, focusing on her. "My mind is on other things."

"After the week you've had, I imagine it is." She was disappointed and a little hurt. It meant so much to her to be in his arms, if only for a dance on a crowded floor. But he was so obviously distracted he scarcely noticed her. At least not in the way she wanted to be noticed.

"Let's go sit down," she said, stifling a sigh when she saw the relief on his face.

"That might be a good idea. Why don't we get something to drink and take it out on the deck?"

Deanna agreed readily, wondering at his restlessness. Was it just the events of the past week on his mind, or was it that'd he'd already had enough of her company?

They found an empty bench in a sheltered nook. Others wandered the deck watching the sparkle of lights from the shore slip by. Voices mingled with the music, punctuated by bursts of laughter.

Deanna sat back, sipping her drink. Lee appeared lost in thought.

"What is it, Lee?" she asked finally.

"What's what?"

Deanna smiled. "You're a thousand miles away. What are you thinking about?"

He leaned back on the bench, his arm brushing hers. A finger tapped against the side of his glass. "I want to ask you something," he said after a long moment.

"So ask."

"I'm not so sure I should."

"Why not?"

"I don't know how you'll react."

"Now I'm really curious," she said. "Go on—ask."

"All right." He took a deep breath and turned to look at her, the ship's lights glinting in his eyes. "Deanna, I want you to hear me out and think about this before you say anything, but...will you marry me?"

Deanna's whole body jerked with shock. She sat upright and stared at him, wide-eyed and speechless.

Lee's lips twisted in wry smile. "I know it's the last thing you expected to hear, but I'm serious."

Deanna found her voice. "Because of Mickey, right?"

"Of course," he said, as though there could be no other reason.

"Did your lawyer suggest this?" It was hard to keep the sarcasm out of her tone.

"She did say it would help," he admitted. "But Mickey depends on both of us, Deanna, and she sees us caring for her—together. You know as well as I do she'll be heartbroken when you move away."

It was all too easy to imagine Mickey's sad little face when they said goodbye. Lee wasn't playing fair. But still, his proposal was out of the question. Not if he wanted her just for Mickey. Frowning, she shook her head. "Lee...this is crazy."

"Is it? I think we could make a good home for Mickey."

"There's more to marriage than making a home for an orphaned child, Lee. Think about it."

"I have," he said. "*You* think about it. No more part-time jobs to cover the rent and other expenses. Just lots of writing time once Mickey's back in school."

"People don't get married for those reasons, Lee. What about...about us?"

Lee reached up to trail his fingers down her cheek, smiling when she jerked back involuntarily. "Oh, I think we'll find something in it for us," he said. He laughed softly at the look on her face, then leaned forward and kissed her.

His lips barely touched hers, but she felt their heat. She couldn't turn away. Desire flared in her and she returned the kiss, her lips parting under gentle pressure. And then he pulled back.

She stared at him, her eyes wide and luminous, wanting more, a lot more. As she opened her mouth to speak, he put a finger against her lips and shook his head.

"Think about it," he said softly, tracing the outline of her mouth.

She could only nod.

IT WAS OUT of the question of course, and she should have told him so right away.

Instead, she'd agreed to think about it, and now she would have to at least pretend to consider his proposal.

Proposal, she thought wryly, slowly getting ready for bed. It had been more of a business proposition, with Lee careful to point out benefits for all sides. Mickey would have two caring guardians. Lee would stand a better chance of retaining custody, thereby keeping his promise to his sister. Deanna would be able to concentrate on her writing. It was a deal in which everyone would gain. To Lee, it was a practical plan.

And yet... Sighing, Deanna sat heavily on the edge of her bed, wondering if that was all it was to him. It had to be. If he cared for her—loved her—he would have said so.

Deanna turned off the bedside lamp and leaned back against the headboard. She brought her knees up and clasped her hands around them, staring off into the dark corners of the room. She knew she should give Lee a flat-out no to his proposal. Anything else was madness—wasn't it? She smiled a little ruefully, knowing she wasn't nearly as resolute as she should be.

It came down to remaining alone or sharing her life with Lee and Mickey. Even without love, Lee could give her companionship, and she'd at least have a chance for happiness.

Lee and Mickey needed her, and she had so much to give.

DEANNA PUSHED through the beaded curtain in the rear of the flower shop. "Hi, Pat," she said.

Pat looked up from the arrangement she was working on. "Hi, Deanna," she greeted her warmly. "It's about time you dropped in. I've phoned a couple of times to find out how things were going, but you're always out."

"I've been next door a lot," Deanna explained. "It's been so hot lately we've been spending most of our time by the pool."

"We?" Pat asked, eyebrows rising.

"Mickey and I," Deanna answered. She picked up a discarded rose and brushed it against her bottom lip.

"What about the uncle?"

"Lee? Oh, he's around—quite a bit, actually. He took me out last night," she added casually.

Pat's eyes widened. "And?"

Deanna put down the rose. "That's what I want to talk to you about. Have you got time?"

"Are you kidding? For this I've got all the time in the world. Listen, I'm overdue for a coffee break. Why don't we go next door and grab a cup?"

"Are you sure?"

"Absolutely. From the look on your face, this has to be a good one."

"It is."

"Great. I need some excitement in my life, vicarious or not. I'll just get my purse and tell Kendra I'm going."

They settled in a balcony table at the restaurant. When they'd been served, Pat leaned forward unexpectantly.

"Well?"

Deanna smiled. Pat had an insatiable curiosity about other people's lives, but Deanna had found her to be a good listener. Right now she needed that.

"Lee proposed to me last night," she stated flatly.

Pat was as shocked as Deanna had been. "What!"

Deanna couldn't help but enjoy the look on her friend's face. "Just what I said. He proposed to me."

"I didn't know you two were that serious. Deanna! You've been holding out!"

Deanna had to laugh. "It's not like it sounds, Pat." She told Pat about Wade Wescott. "Lee wants to keep Mickey," she finished, "and his lawyer's assured him that having a wife will strengthen his case."

"Oh." Pat's disappointment was obvious. "You said no, of course."

"Not yet. He wanted me to think about it."

"But you will say no, won't you?" Pat asked in consternation. "Or... have you fallen in love with him?"

Deanna hesitated, then nodded slowly. She had. There was no longer any point in denying it. Her attraction to Lee had blossomed into love.

"Then what's the problem? Ah... is he in love with you?"

"Not so you'd notice," Deanna said dryly.

"Then why are you even considering this?"

"I don't know. I've gone over it in my mind a hundred times since last night. Part of me says no loud and clear, but..." Deanna sighed and shook her head. "It threw me,

Pat. It was the last thing I expected, and I should have said no right away, but he asked me to think about it, and the more I do..." Her voice trailed off and she picked up her coffee cup.

Pat looked at her shrewdly. "You really want to say yes, don't you?"

"Yeah, I guess I do." Deanna put her cup back down and looked at Pat with a hint of defiance in her eyes.

"Without his love? You know it won't feel complete. Something will always be missing."

"I'm going to feel that way, anyway, without him—them—in my life. I lost everything once, Pat, and it's horrible to be alone when it's not by choice. Maybe I should take what I can. This has to be better than nothing."

"Maybe it will be," Pat said gently. She clasped Deanna's hand.

"You know, Pat, I was up most of the night thinking things over. And it just doesn't seem so bad. I love him—and Mickey, too. She's a wonderful child, and she really needs me in her life right now. It feels good to be needed."

"You can be Mickey's friend without marrying Lee," Pat objected.

"But what if her father tries for custody? We have no guarantees he won't get her."

"But what about *you*—you and Lee?"

Deanna remembered how Lee had answered that question last night. Her lips tingled ever so slightly. "I love him. He's fun to be with and he's very good with Mickey. He'd make a great father, Pat, and I want children very much. Really, when you think about it, it would be quite a good arrangement."

Pat looked as though she didn't believe what she was hearing. "I'm not so sure, Deanna. You're thinking with your head here, instead of your heart."

"No," Deanna said slowly. "If I was using my head, I wouldn't be considering it at all."

"Are you going to say yes?"

Deanna raised her shoulders in a shrug. "I don't know, Pat. I really don't know."

IT WAS TWILIGHT when at last she went next door. She slipped in through the back gate and crossed the lawn to the house. Lee was sitting on the deck, cradling a drink in his hands, his shoulders slouched and his legs stretched out in front of him.

"Hi," she said softly.

His head shot up and he stared at her.

Her stomach clenched nervously. "I hope I'm not disturbing you, but . . . we've got to talk."

"I've been waiting for you," he said, his voice low and without expression. "Come and sit down."

Deanna sat on the lawn chair opposite him. She crossed her ankles and smoothed her skirt with damp palms.

"Would you like a drink?" he asked.

"Yes, please," she answered, flicking her tongue across dry lips.

"Sangria?" There was a pitcher and an empty glass on the table beside him. He'd been expecting her.

"That would be nice, thank you."

He sat up to pour her drink. "It's not strong," he said, passing her a glass already dewy with condensation.

"I wouldn't mind if it was," she murmured and managed a smile. "Is Mickey in bed?"

He nodded. "Fast asleep. We had a pretty full day."

"What did you do?" She hated the stilted sound of her voice. For the first time in a long while, she found it difficult to talk to him.

"I took her in to the office for a couple of hours . . . then we spent the afternoon going through her mother's things.

I'd had them shipped to the company after—" He broke off. "It wasn't easy, Deanna," he admitted roughly, rubbing the back of his neck.

"I don't suppose it was," she said softly. "But it had to be done, and it was good that you could do it together. How is she?"

"Okay now. There were a lot of tears, but they were—I don't know—cleansing, I guess."

Deanna knew the tears hadn't all been Mickey's. "I'm glad. It helps the healing."

He looked at her, his eyes heavy-lidded and brooding. "Did it help you?"

"It took me a long time to get to that point," she admitted. "I couldn't even bear to clear out our apartment. My family had to do it. But once I was able to sort through his things, even give some of them away, I felt as though I'd taken a big step, as though the worst was over."

It wasn't what she had come to talk to him about, but it was good to know she could.

"And was it?"

She tilted her head to one side and answered slowly, "The . . . the rawness, yes. But the rest—missing him, wanting him—took longer. A lot longer. The wounds will always be there, I suppose. They just don't hurt as much after a while."

Silence fell between them, and he studied her face closely, before his eyes became shuttered. He stood up and took a few restless steps, his hands deep in the pockets of his cotton slacks. Then he stopped and turned. "Did you think about what I asked you last night?"

"Almost nonstop," Deanna admitted. She felt nervous and unsure. His hovering didn't help.

"And?"

It was too dark to see his face clearly, but she heard the tension in his voice. She took a deep breath and the words rushed out. "I can't, Lee," she said, shaking her head. "I'm sorry. I wish it was possible, but ... I can't." Her voice was soft, pleading for understanding.

"I see," he said flatly. He sat back down again. "Is there anything I can say to make you change your mind?"

She sighed. *Tell me you love me,* she thought. "No," she said.

"Then that's that." He picked up his glass and took a swallow of the icy liquid.

Deanna's heart gave a little flutter. His words sounded so final. "Can we still be friends?"

He smiled unexpectedly and reached to take her hand. "Of course," he said with surprising gentleness. He rubbed his thumb over her knuckles. "Don't worry about it, Deanna. I didn't want to upset you. It just seemed worth a try."

"I'm sorry," she said again, her heart swelling with love at the tenderness in his touch. "I wish I could, for Mickey." *For you.* "I really do."

"I know. I'd like it to be different, but I do understand. I'll win this one on my own." He released her hand and sat back.

Deanna took a nervous sip from her glass. It would have been easier to face his anger than this gentle understanding. For a moment she was tempted to tell him she had changed her mind. That, yes, she would marry him.

"I should go," she said suddenly, standing up. It was hard to sit quietly, knowing she had disappointed him. "I'd like to write a bit tonight." That was an excuse. She knew she wouldn't be able to pen a word.

He nodded and rose to his feet. "Deanna ..."

She turned back, her eyebrows raised in query.

He put a hand on her shoulder and drew her to him, holding her lightly in his arms. He smiled, then touched his lips to hers.

Passion hit Deanna like a slap. Her arms went around his neck and she pressed closer, welcoming his deepening kiss with parted lips. His tongue met hers, and she sagged against him with a moan of desire. His hands cupped her hips and pulled her tight to his and she felt his arousal. For a white-hot moment, she wanted nothing but to lie with him, their bodies entwined . . .

He pulled back suddenly, leaving her staring at him, wide-eyed and breathless. His eyes seemed to glow with need as he let out a ragged breath and stepped away.

"Are you sure you won't marry me?" he asked harshly.

Emotions churned in a painful mixture that showed in her eyes. She made a move toward him, then shook her head violently. With a hand pressed to her mouth, she turned and fled.

CHAPTER NINE

DEANNA ENDURED another night of fitful sleep. Every time she closed her eyes she saw Lee's face, felt his arms around her, his lips on hers. She wanted him so much, in every way.

If only he could return her love.

Deanna was up early. She poured herself a cup of coffee and went to sit at the table, watching the budgies chatter to each other. Sighing tiredly, she rubbed at the line between her brows.

It had been hard to turn Lee down. She couldn't help but be tempted by the picture of the three of them forming a family, even adding to it in a year or so. It would mean so much to Mickey. And the thought of no longer being alone was—

The doorbell pealed suddenly, much to the delight of the birds. Their chirping increased excitedly as they side-stepped along the perch.

Deanna put down her cup and went to answer the door.

Mickey was there, wide-eyed and grinning. "Deanna!" She flung herself into Deanna's arms and clung tightly. "I'm so happy," she said, her voice muffled in the curve of Deanna's shoulder.

Deanna held the girl closely. "Why, sweetie?" she asked.

"You and Uncle Lee. You get to be my aunt just like I wished!" Mickey pulled back, her eyes sparkling. "I was feeling really bad this morning because I missed my mom so much yesterday. Then I heard Uncle Lee on the phone saying he was going to get married!" She sighed tremulously and snuggled back into Deanna's arms. "It's just perfect."

Deanna straightened in shock. What in the world was Lee up to? Then she saw him hurrying through her gate, and she stared, openmouthed. He had done this to force her hand? He wouldn't dare, would he?

Her mouth closed and her lips tightened into a thin line as he approached. She started to speak, then stopped. She couldn't tell Lee what she thought of him in front of Mickey. The poor kid. How dared he raise her hopes like that? She glared angrily at him.

He stood there, leaning against the front-porch railing, saying nothing.

Deanna gave Mickey a hug, then set her back. "The cats are round back, sweetie," she said, her voice carefully controlled. "Why don't you go see if they want in? They haven't had their breakfast yet."

"Okay," Mickey said cheerfully. She grinned at her uncle before spinning around to go through the house to the back.

Deanna crossed her arms over her chest, her face set and cold. "Explain yourself."

He shrugged and had the grace to look a little ashamed. "I was talking to Wescott. He makes me so damned angry, Deanna, with his threats and posturing it was out before I knew it. I guess I hoped it would make him back off. I didn't know Mickey was listening until I heard her squealing with delight and saw her running off." He smiled sheepishly. "She was over here before I could stop her to explain. I'm sorry, Deanna, but maybe we could let it ride for a bit."

Deanna gave her head an emphatic shake. "I hardly think so. Lee, this isn't just a promise to take her to the beach or buy her a new bike. I said no last night and I meant it. We can't let her go on thinking otherwise."

He stared at her, his eyes dark. "Are you sure?"

Deanna forced herself to look directly at him, raising her chin defiantly. "You saw her Lee—she's ecstatic! She thinks it's all arranged, that we're all going to be together in a happy little home for ever and ever! It's not fair to let her go on thinking that way.''

Lee scowled at her in obvious frustration. "You thought about saying yes, Deanna. I know you did. Are you sure you know what you really want?''

"I know I don't want to be coerced into anything, Lee Stratton." It was already too late to get out of this without hurting Mickey, and the thought of the child's disappointment caused her a sharp pang.

"Wescott was partying when he called," Lee said abruptly. "Even this early in the morning. He made it clear he wanted Mickey for the day. I said no, flat out. Not after last time, and certainly not while he was drinking. He said he was seeing a lawyer this afternoon."

Deanna's anger disappeared in a flash. "Oh, no! Not so soon."

"Oh, yes," Lee said grimly. "He's on a power trip, Deanna. He got money out of me, but that's not enough. He wants to beat me. He doesn't give a damn about Mickey. It's me he wants to get at."

He took his hands from his pockets and tiredly rubbed the back of his neck. "I've got to be able to prove that I can give Mickey the best possible home. I'm sure I can win, even without you, Deanna—but it would help if you were part of the plan."

Deanna's sigh was one of regret and frustration. "It probably would, Lee, but—"

He held up a hand to stop her. "I'll make sure it's not a sacrifice on your part." There was a note of determination in his voice. "The company is beginning to pay back quite well—there'll be money for anything you want. I really think that once you're comfortable with the idea, you'll find it suitable."

Deanna was shaking her head. "Comfortable" and "suitable" were not the words she associated with getting married. *Tell me you love me, Lee,* she thought with a sinking heart. *That'll make everything right.*

"It doesn't have to be forever—just long enough to see this thing through. If you want out later, fine. Say yes, Deanna," he coaxed. "For Mickey's sake, if nothing else."

Nothing else.... She wanted everything, and she wanted forever. How could she settle for what he was offering?

"Say yes, Deanna," he repeated softly. "For Mickey."

"You fight dirty," she whispered.

One corner of his mouth lifted in a smile. "Is that a yes?"

She stared down at the floorboards, arms still crossed and pressed tightly to her stomach.

She should be furious with Lee for using her love for Mickey to get his own way, but all she felt was a curious calm. She might not like his tactics, but his motives were true. His heart was in the right place.

She could understand his determination that Mickey not suffer any more than she already had, that he keep his promise to his sister. She raised her eyes and looked at him in solemn reflection.

"On one condition," she said finally.

He flashed a smile that was full of confidence. "Name it."

Maybe he couldn't give her the love she wanted, but there was one thing he *could* give her.

Her chin jutted out defiantly. "I don't want your money. I want...a child."

No shock or surprise showed on his face. Instead, his smile widened and his eyes glinted. "No problem," he said softly. He leaned forward and brushed her lips with his. "No problem at all."

He wrapped a lock of her hair around his finger, watching a mix of expressions chase across her face. "It'll be all right, Deanna," he said gently.

Her eyes were filled with uncertainty. "Will it?"

"Yes," he said with conviction. "Now. Let's collect Mickey. I'll take you out for breakfast before I go to the office."

Deanna followed him slowly into the house to the kitchen, wondering at herself. She could have gotten out of this. She could have told Mickey the truth. Mickey would have been upset, but that wouldn't have lasted.

She had given in so easily, with almost none of the anger she had every right to feel, as though she was glad to have the decision made for her.

It wouldn't be so bad, she told herself. She loved Mickey and wanted her to be happy. And as far as Lee went... Her stomach gave a peculiar twist. Maybe he would come to care for her, at least a little....

Mickey looked at them as they entered the kitchen, and she grinned delightedly. "I just thought of something—Alfie and Imp and Leo *and* the birds get to move in, too!"

"Oh, great," Lee said with a grimace.

"Isn't it?" Deanna said. She felt her spirits lift. Just seeing the happiness shining in Mickey's eyes made everything seem all right, at least for the moment. "You know," she added, tossing a look at Lee, "I've been thinking about getting a dog. Or two."

"Yeah!" Mickey jumped up and down. "That'd be neat. A poodle and a—a beagle!"

Deanna grinned at the look on Lee's face. "We could call them Mitzi and—"

"And Fred! Can we Uncle Lee? Please?"

"No," Lee said mildly. "But if you stop making like a pogo stick, I'll take you out for breakfast."

"Strawberry waffles?"

"Whatever you want. But we've got to get going. I have to be in the office by eleven."

"Okay! Let's go! Oh, I fed the cats, Deanna," Mickey said over her shoulder as she trotted down the hall to the front door.

Lee stood watching her for a moment, then glanced at the cats and the birds. He looked ruefully at Deanna and slowly shook his head. "All this and babies, too," he murmured.

Deanna lifted her chin and perused him coolly. "Serves you right," she said, and followed Mickey to the door.

THAT EVENING Deanna closed the back gate and walked quietly across the yard. Lee and Mickey were sitting at a patio table, an open book between them. Deanna watched them for a moment, her heart giving a little leap. For better or for worse, they were going to be a family.

"Hi," she called, skirting the pool. "What are you reading?" she asked as she came up to them, carrying a gift-wrapped package.

"Your book," Mickey said. "Uncle Lee wanted me to tell him the neat parts so Dave can make a game about it."

Lee smiled at Deanna as she sat down. "He can't incorporate all the settings, so he asked me to find out which ones Mickey likes best. He's enthusiastic about this, Deanna. It could turn out to be quite a popular little game."

"Great," she said lightly.

"I told him he has to put in the part where Tasha rides on the rainbow dragon to get away from the slug people and they have to pick the right waterfall, the one with the jeweled cave that leads to freedom. Only they have to get through the lab... lab... What's that word again?"

"Labyrinth," Lee and Deanna said in unison.

Mickey grinned at them. "Yeah, that. Anyway, that's a neat part. It would be fun in a game." She eyed the package Deanna had set on the table. "What's that?" she asked casually.

Deanna smiled. "It's for you, sweetie. Open it."

Mickey made short work of the paper. "It's your new book!"

"I just got the advance copies today. I thought you'd like one."

"I do! Thanks, Deanna. I can't wait to start reading it."

"I seem to remember when you found reading boring," Deanna teased.

"That was before. I like it now."

"Well," Lee said, glancing at his watch, "why don't you go get ready for bed? You can read until you feel sleepy."

"Okay," Mickey agreed readily. She got up, clutching both books to her chest. Turning back suddenly, she flashed a cheeky grin. "I guess you two want to be alone, huh, now that you're going to get married?"

"I guess we do," Lee said. "Go to bed, kid."

"I'm going, I'm going." She blew a kiss their way, then skipped into the house, giggling.

Smiling, Lee watched her leave. "You know, when Teri was telling me what Mickey was like, she said she was as sweet as sugar and as sassy as spice."

"That's Mickey, all right," Deanna said, delighted with the description. She was silent for a moment, then asked, "Did you get much of a chance to talk to Teri before...before she died?"

"We had a few days," Lee said. "She was pretty weak, but we were able to talk. Mainly about Mickey. I think by that point the worse thing for her was knowing she wouldn't live to see Mickey grow up."

Deanna thought of Lee, watching her sister die. She knew too well the helplessness and anger he must have felt. "It was hard, wasn't it?" she said softly, remembering the last days with Ryan.

"Yes," he said, and they shared a look of mutual sympathy. "She talked a lot about what she wanted for Mickey's future, but it wasn't about careers or the choices she might make. She just wanted her to be happy. Lord knows she had little enough of that herself."

"Mickey's going to do okay," Deanna said confidently.

"If we can keep her away from that damn father of hers," Lee responded grimly.

"Have you heard from him again?"

"Not a word. His last call was just a bluff. He'll go through the money before he does anything." He paused. "Deanna, thank you for going along with me this morning. I know we could probably have set Mickey straight without hurting her too much, but I want to be able to present a real family to the courts, should it come to that. I feel this is the best way to go."

"Maybe it is," she said. "All I know is that I don't want Mickey to have to go live with her father. It would be disastrous."

Lee studied Deanna in silence, slanting rays from the setting sun glinting on the gold in his hair. "Then you will marry me?" he asked, his eyes intent.

Deanna looked down at her clasped hands. "I said I would," she murmured.

"But you have doubts."

"Of course I do," she said, glancing up at him. She remembered the excitement and wonder of the night she and Ryan had fallen in love. The joy with which they had made plans to share their lives.

That was what she wanted with Lee, more than anything else in the world. What was it going to do to her, learning to be content with what affection he could give her? Would there come a day when she would no longer be able to bear living with him, knowing he didn't return her love?

"This isn't exactly a normal situation, is it?" she asked, unable to keep the longing from her voice.

"You mean, we're not in love," he said flatly.

You're not in love, she thought wistfully. "People usually are when they decide to get married."

"And how many of them end up divorced within a few years? We'll go into this with our eyes open, Deanna. There won't be any surprises."

Oh, there'd be surprises all right, Deanna thought with conviction. Lee was not a staid, boring man. "What if you fall in love with someone else? It could happen."

"I won't," Lee said with quiet certainty. "What about you?"

Deanna shook her head slowly. "I won't."

Silence fell between them, and she knew he thought she still loved Ryan. She would let him think that way, for now.

With a set face, Lee watched Deanna as she stared across the pool into the shadowy recesses of the yard. Finally he got up and held out his hand to her.

"Come here."

Almost reluctantly, Deanna put her hand in his and let him pull her to her feet. She didn't resist when he took her into his arms.

He held her, gently stroking her hair, watching her face in the fading sunlight. "It feels right to me, Deanna," he said softly. "All of it. We'll be okay."

He smoothed the frown from her brow and brushed his lips over hers, then claimed them in a kiss.

Deanna leaned against him, letting his kiss carry her away. He pulled her closer and her body molded to his, giving in to its exquisite demands. It had been so long, she thought dazedly. So very long...

Passion threatened to overwhelm her and she felt a sudden flash of panic, knowing she could lose herself in his arms. Gasping, she pushed away, alarm showing clearly on her face.

"Stop. Please stop." She desperately needed to maintain some control.

Frowning, Lee kept a hand on her arm, preventing her from turning away. "What's wrong, Deanna?" he asked roughly.

She looked at him, saw the pulse throb in the side of his neck and shook her head. How could she explain her vulnerability without telling him how much she loved him? Those were not words he wanted to hear.

She pulled away and wrapped her arms around herself, then stared out over the yard.

"I need . . . I need time," she whispered. Time to come to terms with the fact that he would marry her without loving her, that his attraction to her was purely a physical thing, lacking the lasting strength of love.

Lee came up behind her. Tense and aroused, he took her in his arms. She stayed purposely stiff, fighting the urge to relax against him and let his stirring caresses carry her away.

He turned her around until she had no choice but to look at him. Her eyes were wide, glistening with emotion, and she put her hands to his chest, pushing back just a bit.

"How much time are you going to need?" His voice was soft but demanding, and he stared at her mouth as though he longed to claim it again.

Deanna looked down at her hands splayed against his white cotton shirt and shook her head. "I don't know." How long would it take to toughen her heart, to protect herself from the knowledge that he didn't return her love?

His hands made one long stroke down her back to cup her bottom and pull her closer to him. He smiled at the little gasp that escaped her lips.

Her legs felt weak and her fingers curled, then clung to him for support. She closed her eyes, biting her bottom lip as he nuzzled the warm skin below her ear. Sensation so sharp it was almost painful shot down her neck.

"Lee, please—please stop."

Taking a ragged breath, Lee raised his head, staring at her with eyes heavy with desire. He released her abruptly and stepped away, then began to pace the deck.

"I'm sorry," Deanna said, watching him. "I . . . I don't mean to tease. It's just . . . I can't. Not yet."

Lee stopped his pacing and turned to her. His body was taut, his face set in rigid lines. "It's because of him, isn't it? Your husband. It's him you want, not me."

She hugged herself tightly. Ryan had never been further from her thoughts.

"But you can't have him, so you'll settle for me," Lee continued flatly. "You'll have a home, a husband, children—but inside you'll always be wishing it was him."

"That's not true, Lee," she said quietly. "I would never do that."

"No?" It was obvious he didn't believe her.

"Lee, I'm just asking for a bit of time before we . . . before we go any further. I don't think that's unreasonable under the circumstances. You pushed me into this. Give me the time I need to come to terms with it."

Lee stared at her, his face an unreadable mask. Then, sighing wearily, he nodded. "All right, I'll wait. If it's time you need, you've got it. But it isn't going to be easy. I want you, Deanna," he added, his voice deep and ragged, "and I want you right now. Maybe you'd better go."

Deanna hesitated, hating to leave him like this, but after a moment she turned and walked away. It was probably the wisest thing to do.

She glanced over her shoulder, but he had his back to her.

"Good night," she called softly, but heard no response. Biting her bottom lip, she hurried home.

DEANNA SAT ON THE EDGE of her bed holding the picture of Ryan in her hands. She got up slowly and went to the closet to take down a small box filled with mementos of her past. She untied the faded ribbon and removed the top. Without bothering to look at the contents, she placed the picture gently inside, then closed the box again and put it away. It was her final goodbye.

For so many years the picture had been the first thing she saw in the morning and the last thing at night.

Now things had changed. She would marry Lee, and it would be his face she saw, on the pillow beside hers. It would be Lee who reached for her in the night, kissed and caressed her, made love to her. He would be her husband.

But he wouldn't love her. The realization was painful. She would live with the fear that he could fall in love with someone else at any time...or stay married to her, content enough, but never loving her. The first would devastate her. The second would wear her down with useless longing.

Was there a third possibility? Would the physical attraction he felt for her eventually grow into love? She would have to cling to that hope. Without it, she knew she could never go through with this marriage.

She went to kneel by the window. The light from Lee's bedroom slanted across the deck, and she wondered what kept him awake. Was he working or pacing the floor, thinking about how his circumstances had changed?

A few weeks ago he had no one dependent on him, no cares except his business. Now he had a deathbed promise to keep. And he would keep it, to the best of his ability, even if that meant marrying her to give Mickey a proper home.

THE NEXT MORNING Lee stood in front of her on her doorstep, hands in the pockets of his cotton slacks. He was frowning, the green light in his eyes subdued.

"Deanna," he said abruptly, "we've got to talk."

"Where's Mickey?" she asked, leading the way into the living room.

"She's watching Peter Pan on the VCR," he said, following her. "She'll be all right for a while."

Deanna took a seat, but Lee remained standing, hands still in his pockets as he stared broodingly at her.

"What's the matter?" she asked. "Is it Mickey's father again?"

Lee shook his head. "It's you," he said. "Us."

Deanna looked down at her hands. "Oh."

"I did a lot of thinking last night and . . . it's not going to work, Deanna."

Startled, she stared at him. "What?"

"I coerced you into something you aren't ready for," he said. His eyes were dark, his face set.

"You don't want to get married," she said flatly.

He shook his head.

She jumped up, scowling at him. "Damn it, Lee. What the hell are you playing at? I say no, but you manage to let Mickey believe we're getting married, anyway. So, nice person that I am, I go along with it. Now you tell me it's off!"

His face tautened. "Yeah, well, I'm sorry. I can't go through with it."

Deanna stood with her chin raised defiantly, while inside, pain was tearing her apart. "Why not?" she demanded.

The corner of his mouth lifted in a half smile and he came to her, resting his hands on her shoulders.

"It's not you," he said quietly. "Well, maybe in a way it is. I forced you into all this, and . . ." He shook his head. "It's not right."

His nearness softened her anger and replaced it with love and longing. "But, Lee, I wouldn't have gone along with it if I hadn't—"

He stepped back and held up his hand to stop her. "It doesn't matter. I'll tell Mickey. She won't like it, but she'll understand. I'm taking her away for a couple of weeks. It'll give her time to adjust."

There was something so final in his voice. "I will see you again?" she said anxiously.

He rubbed the back of his neck. "It'll be hard to avoid. But maybe you should distance yourself from Mickey. This house will sell as soon as it hits the market, and then where will you be?"

What was going on? Why this abrupt change? "What about Mickey's father?"

He shrugged. "I'll just have to trust that the courts will see that I can give her a better home than he can."

She moved closer and laid a hand on his arm. "We haven't given it much of a chance, Lee. We just need a bit of time to adjust."

He ran a finger along her jaw, then gently over her lips. He stepped away again, his eyes dark and distant.

"It's not time we—I—need, Deanna. I've come to realize I can't go into any half marriage. I want it all." He let out a deep breath. "For what it's worth, I'm sorry." He turned on his heel to leave.

Deanna took a step toward him. "Lee, wait!" But he didn't look back. The door closed firmly behind him.

Stunned, Deanna collapsed into a chair, tears stinging her eyes. He had come to realize he couldn't marry her without love, after all. His attraction to her and his desire to give Mickey a home weren't enough.

And so he had walked out of her life as suddenly as he had come into it.

Tears filled her eyes and flowed down her cheeks. Now she no longer even had the hope that someday he might come to love her. It was bleak and dismal knowledge.

Deanna sat in despair most of the day. By late afternoon, she could stand it no longer. She had to talk to Lee, to find out how Mickey was, if nothing else. She couldn't abruptly cut the child from her life even if Lee thought it was best. Mickey would be hurting and needing to talk.

Heart beating rapidly, she went next door and pressed the doorbell. No answer. She rang again, but the door stayed closed. After hesitating for a moment, she used the key Lee had given her and went inside.

The house was cool and quiet, the light muted by half-drawn vertical blinds. She called out tentatively, her voice seeming to echo in the stillness. There was no one home.

Deanna went to check Mickey's room. A quick look in the closet and dresser drawers showed most of her clothes gone. Despair began to grow anew. Had he really left just like that?

She went to stand in the doorway of his room. It was dim and still, but she felt his presence. Closing her eyes, she took a deep breath and caught the elusive scent that was him. She breathed again and saw his face in her mind's eye.

Tears trickled down her cheeks. Why did he feel he had to leave? They could have worked something out. They could have at least stayed friends.

IT DIDN'T TAKE Deanna long to realize how empty her life was without Lee and Mickey. She was restless and unable to work. By the end of the week, the continued silence from the house next door became unbearable. She wanted them home!

Lee was on her mind, from the time she woke up until she drifted into restless sleep. She tried to write, but couldn't stop thinking about him. The pictures that became words beneath her pen wouldn't form, but she could see Lee's face clearly—the glint of green light in his eyes and the gold-streaked hair that refused to stay in place. She thought of how gentle he could be, then remembered the passion in his kisses. Her hands clenched with tension. How she longed for his touch!

She thought of how positive she'd once been that she would never love again and wished she had been right. The pain of unrequited love struck deep.

He had said that he didn't want a half marriage, that he wanted it all. Why couldn't he want it from her?

As she doodled absently on a piece of paper, a thought struck her. She had let Lee believe she still loved Ryan, that *he* was behind her refusal to allow Lee to make love to her.

Lee had said he didn't want a half marriage. What if he was referring to *her* feelings for him? Was it possible?

She remembered how he had felt in her arms, kissing her passionately, as though he couldn't get close enough to her. She remembered feeling desire shudder through him when she returned his caresses.

And then she had pushed him aside, pleading for time, telling him she wasn't yet ready to accept him as a lover. He had wanted her, wildly, and she had rejected him.

He was used to her being forthright and honest. Of course he would believe she still loved Ryan.

A smile broke through her thoughtful frown, and she jumped up to pace the kitchen, relishing the hope that surged through her. She did a pirouette of excitement, then whistled to the birds, laughing at their chorus of approval.

Sober reflection hit a few moments later.

She was acting as though being honest with Lee about her feelings would mean he would admit to loving her in return. She didn't know that for sure.

But she had to find out.

NEARLY A WEEK AND A HALF passed before Deanna saw any signs of life next door. She had spent the day helping Pat prepare flowers for a wedding and, once home, had gone to the back door to let the cats out. It was then that she heard Mickey's clear voice calling Lee to the phone.

Her heart quickened with nervous anticipation and she licked at lips suddenly dry.

She had missed them so much that she wanted to go to them immediately. But she restrained herself. Later this evening, she told herself firmly.

Time passed slowly. Finally, as the sun began its slow descent, Deanna cut through her yard and around to the back of Lee's. She let herself in through the gate and stood for a moment, watching them.

They were sitting outside on the deck. Lee was reading the paper while Mickey sprawled with the comics on a towel spread on the cedar flooring.

Her heart swelling with love, Deanna took a deep breath and went toward them.

"Hi!" she called out.

Mickey's head shot up and she scrambled to her feet, grinning widely. "Deanna!"

Lee put down the paper, his face suddenly still.

Mickey flung herself into Deanna's arms and, laughing, Deanna hugged her back.

"It's good to see you, sweetie," she said. "Did you have a nice holiday?"

"Yeah. We went to this cottage right by a lake, and there was a boat and everything. I even water-skied! Well, I tried, anyway. It's hard. Uncle Lee did real good, though."

Deanna glanced at Lee. He was sitting upright in his chair, watching them beneath hooded eyes. She smiled uncertainly.

His face relaxed a little as he returned her smile. "Hello, Deanna."

She nodded self-consciously and turned her attention to Mickey, who had a tight hold on her arm. "What else did you do while you were gone?"

Mickey shrugged. "Lotsa stuff. I caught a fish—a jack. It was pretty big, but Uncle Lee said if I wanted to catch fish I had to clean them and eat them." She made a face. "Yuck. So I didn't fish anymore. Oh, and I saw a moose with a baby wading in the water! That was neat."

Deanna smiled at her. "It sounds like you had fun."

"Yeah, but—" Mickey looked up, her eyes wide and serious "—I wished you were there."

"It would have been nice," Deanna said lightly. "But it was good for you and your uncle to have some time together." Deanna looked at Lee, willing him to say something, anything, that would give her an inkling of what he was thinking.

"He said you aren't getting married," Mickey told her in a troubled voice.

Deanna stroked Mickey's hair comfortingly. "I know. But I'd like a chance to talk to him about it," she said, keeping her eyes on Lee's face. She saw a flicker of expression, so brief she might have imagined it.

Mickey's eyes took on a light of hope. She glanced at her uncle, then back to Deanna. "So, should I go play or something?"

"Do you mind?"

"Nope. I can go watch the second *Star Wars* movie. Uncle Lee bought all three of them yesterday on the way home from the lake. We only watched one so far." She grinned at Deanna. "I really want to see it."

Deanna gave her a quick hug. "Thanks, sweetie. I'll talk to you later." She watched Mickey skip to the house and disappear inside. Taking a deep breath, she turned to Lee.

"It sounds as though Mickey had a good time." She sat down on the lawn chair opposite Lee, crossing her ankles as she smoothed her skirt over her knees. "Did you?"

Lee shrugged. "It was all right. Get a lot of writing done?"

Deanna suppressed a sigh. She hated this sort of polite talk between them. "No, actually, I didn't. I couldn't concentrate." She took another deep breath and continued, "I didn't like you leaving me like that, Lee."

He sat there watching her and said nothing.

Deanna looked down at her hands, rubbing a thumb nervously over her knuckles. This was hard, but she wouldn't sit quietly by and let love slip away. Not if there was even the slightest chance that Lee might return some of what she felt for him.

She looked up, her gray eyes wide and vulnerable. It was time to put everything on the line. Life was too short.

"Ryan's been gone for a long time now, Lee. He's . . . a fond memory, that's all. I'm not in love with him anymore."

Lee sat erect, tension radiating from his body. "How can you be sure?"

She smiled softly, encouraged by the look on his face. "Because I know I don't want to live the rest of my life in the past. I want to look ahead, and when I do, I see you and Mickey. I want to share your lives."

Lee stared at her for a long moment. "I need your love, Deanna. All of it. I can't settle for anything less."

She sighed in relief. "Good. Because that's exactly what I need from you." She looked at him, holding nothing back. "I love you, Lee Stratton. I really do."

Lee stood up and came to her, the green in his eyes flashing. He held out his hands.

Deanna put her hands in his, loving the warmth of his touch. She let him pull her to her feet, then looped her arms around his neck, her body relaxing against his. She stroked his hair and smiled serenely.

"Well?" she asked. She saw the love in his face, but wanted the words.

"Well what?"

She gave a soft sigh of exasperation. "Do you love me, will you marry me—simple little things like that."

His eyes searched hers. His answer was a searing kiss that left her breathless and clinging.

"Yes, I do and, yes, I will," he said, his voice thick with curbed passion. He kissed her again, his mouth warm and caressing.

"I missed you," he muttered, holding her tight. "So damned much. It was all I could do to stay away."

Deanna ran her hands across his shoulders, relishing in the feel of his taut strength beneath her fingers. "I missed you, too," she said. "That's what we get for not being honest with each other. But your going away did make me realize just how much I need you in my life . . . and how much I love you."

"Oh, Deanna," he murmured, his mouth moving over her face. "You don't know how much I've longed to hear you say that."

"Show me," she whispered.

"I'd like to," he said hoarsely. "But we have a very curious little girl who could very well decide to come and see if we're getting it right this time." He cupped the back of her head and stroked her hair.

"I love you, Deanna, and I want you in my life." He smiled into her eyes. "Marry me, and soon."

Deanna's eyes closed against a sudden wash of tears, and she nodded. Blinking, she looked at him and smiled tremulously. "As soon as possible," she whispered. "I love you so much." She found his lips and kissed him.

Mickey looked out the kitchen door and saw their embrace. "All right!" she exclaimed and came running toward them.

IT WAS LATE. Already the eastern sky held a hint of light, and a lone robin began a tentative song. Cool air spiced with the scent of dew-washed flowers wafted into Lee's room.

It had been a wonderful night of lovemaking, full of discovery and delight. In Lee's embrace there had been no room for memories.

Deanna turned in his arms, relishing the feel of his body against hers. She smiled contentedly and snuggled closer, running a hand over his shoulder.

He stirred and she kissed him softly. "I should be going," she murmured.

"Mmm? Why?" he asked sleepily.

"Before Mickey gets up."

Lee pulled her closer, cradling her head on his shoulder. "She won't mind if you're here."

"I know." Deanna stroked his chest, loving the feel of his smooth skin beneath her fingers. "But...I'd rather. I'll feel more comfortable."

"If you must. But before you go..."

His kiss was slow and sleepy, full of warmth and love. Deanna pressed against him, reveling in the touch of his hands.

"I love you, Deanna," Lee murmured against the warm skin of her neck.

"And I love you," Deanna returned softly, stroking his hair back from his forehead. She snuggled down in his arms smiling in contentment.

"How soon can we get married?" Lee asked.

"The sooner the better," Deanna said. "We can start planning tomorrow—today," she corrected, glancing at the brightening window. She stretched, her body moving easily against his . "I should be going," she said again, but with considerably less conviction.

"Stay awhile," Lee said, tightening his hold.

"All right," Deanna agreed readily. If it wasn't for wanting to maintain a sense of decorum for Mickey's sake, she would stay where she was until morning.

They lay in silence for a few moments, sleepily content just to hold each other.

"I hate to bring this up," Deanna said eventually, "but have you heard from Mickey's father lately?" There'd been no opportunity to talk about it before.

"Not a word," Lee said. "I give him another couple of months to go through the money, then he'll be sniffing around again hoping to get more. But I'll call his bluff next time."

"What if he tries the courts?"

"No one will think for an instant that he can give Mickey a better home than we can. And she'll want to stay with us. That counts for a lot."

He kissed her. "Deanna, I think you should know that I was head over heels in love with you the first time I proposed—that I didn't ask you just for Mickey's sake. I wanted you for myself." He pulled her close and kissed her again.

"Even without Mickey, I'd have wanted you," he murmured against her lips. "I've been under your spell from the moment I saw you scrambling over that wall, all long, long legs and big, gray eyes."

"Well, you certainly fooled me," she said. "You scared me half to death. I thought you were one right cranky neighbor. But," she added with a kiss to his jaw, "not without your attractions." She nestled her head in the hollow of his shoulder, and he stroked her hair.

"I'm glad we're going to be a family," he said. "The three of us belong together."

Deanna nodded, her cheek brushing against his chest. "We do, don't we?" She ran a hand over his side and down his thigh. "But does it have to be just three of us? I was thinking a couple more family members might be nice."

"I'll assume you're not talking about—what was it?—a poodle and a beagle?" Lee asked dryly.

Deanna lifted her head and smiled at him. "You got that right. Remember, you've already promised, and I think Mickey might prefer a cousin or two over a couple of dogs, don't you?"

"Absolutely," Lee said with conviction. "Are you talking right away here?"

"Oh...I think maybe a bit of practice is called for first." She caressed his back, relishing the feel of his skin. His muscles rippled beneath her hands as he pulled her under him.

"Practice away," he murmured, his mouth finding hers in a kiss of growing passion.

He lifted his head and pushed back for a moment, looking at her, his eyes heavy with feeling. "I love you, Deanna," he said. "I'm so thankful you came into my life."

Deanna's eyes blurred with tears of joy. "Oh, Lee," she whispered. "You make me so happy. I love you so very much."

She pulled him to her and kissed him, savoring the wonder of his love.

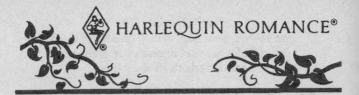

HARLEQUIN ROMANCE®

WELCOME BACK, MARGARET WAY!

After an absence of five years, Margaret Way—one of our
most popular authors ever—returns to Romance!

Start the New Year with the excitement and passion of

ONE FATEFUL SUMMER
A brand-new Romance
from Margaret Way

Available in January wherever Harlequin Books are sold.

HRMW

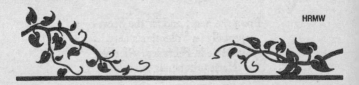

**Fifty red-blooded, white-hot, true-blue hunks
from every State in the Union!**

Look for MEN MADE IN AMERICA! Written by some
of our most poplar authors, these stories feature fifty of
the strongest, sexiest men, each from a different state in
the union!

Two titles available every other month at your favorite
retail outlet.

In January, look for:

DREAM COME TRUE by Ann Major (Florida)
WAY OF THE WILLOW by Linda Shaw (Georgia)

In March, look for:

TANGLED LIES by Anne Stuart (Hawaii)
ROGUE'S VALLEY by Kathleen Creighton (Idaho)

You won't be able to resist MEN MADE IN AMERICA!

POSTCARDS FROM EUROPE

HARLEQUIN PRESENTS®

HPPFE2

Travel across Europe in 1994 with
Harlequin Presents. Collect a new
Postcards From Europe title each month!

Don't miss
MASK OF DECEPTION
by Sara Wood
Harlequin Presents #1628

Available in February wherever
Harlequin Presents books are sold.

Hi—
It's carnival time in
Italy! The streets of
Venice are filled
with music—the
costumes are
incredible. And
I can't wait to
tell you about
Lucenzo Salviati...
Love, Meredith

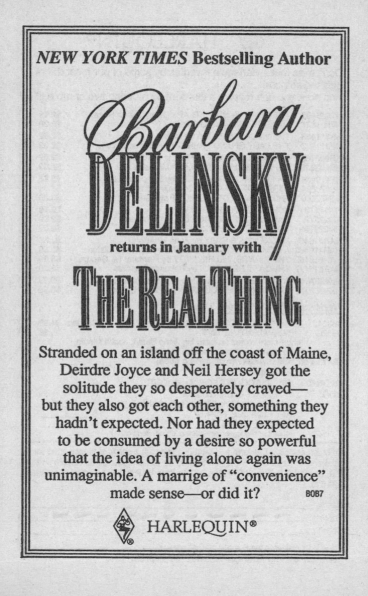

·HARLEQUIN®

Don't miss these Harlequin favorites by some of our most distin-
guished authors!
And now, you can receive a discount by ordering two or more titles!

HT#25409	THE NIGHT IN SHINING ARMOR by JoAnn Ross	$2.99	☐
HT#25471	LOVESTORM by JoAnn Ross	$2.99	☐
HP#11463	THE WEDDING by Emma Darcy	$2.89	☐
HP#11592	THE LAST GRAND PASSION by Emma Darcy	$2.99	☐
HR#03188	DOUBLY DELICIOUS by Emma Goldrick	$2.89	☐
HR#03248	SAFE IN MY HEART by Leigh Michaels	$2.89	☐
HS#70464	CHILDREN OF THE HEART by Sally Garrett	$3.25	☐
HS#70524	STRING OF MIRACLES by Sally Garrett	$3.39	☐
HS#70500	THE SILENCE OF MIDNIGHT by Karen Young	$3.39	☐
HI#22178	SCHOOL FOR SPIES by Vickie York	$2.79	☐
HI#22212	DANGEROUS VINTAGE by Laura Pender	$2.89	☐
HI#22219	TORCH JOB by Patricia Rosemoor	$2.89	☐
HAR#16459	MACKENZIE'S BABY by Anne McAllister	$3.39	☐
HAR#16466	A COWBOY FOR CHRISTMAS by Anne McAllister	$3.39	☐
HAR#16462	THE PIRATE AND HIS LADY by Margaret St. George	$3.39	☐
HAR#16477	THE LAST REAL MAN by Rebecca Flanders	$3.39	☐
HH#28704	A CORNER OF HEAVEN by Theresa Michaels	$3.99	☐
HH#28707	LIGHT ON THE MOUNTAIN by Maura Seger	$3.99	☐

Harlequin Promotional Titles

#83247	YESTERDAY COMES TOMORROW by Rebecca Flanders	$4.99	☐
#83257	MY VALENTINE 1993	$4.99	

(short-story collection featuring Anne Stuart, Judith Arnold,
Anne McAllister, Linda Randall Wisdom)
(limited quantities available on certain titles)

	AMOUNT	$	
DEDUCT:	10% DISCOUNT FOR 2+ BOOKS	$	
ADD:	POSTAGE & HANDLING	$	
	($1.00 for one book, 50¢ for each additional)		
	APPLICABLE TAXES*	$	_____
	TOTAL PAYABLE	$	_____
	(check or money order—please do not send cash)		

To order, complete this form and send it, along with a check or money order for the
total above, payable to Harlequin Books, to: **In the U.S.:** 3010 Walden Avenue,
P.O. Box 9047, Buffalo, NY 14269-9047; **In Canada:** P.O. Box 613, Fort Erie, Ontario,
L2A 5X3.

Name: _____

Address: _____ City: _____

State/Prov.: _____ Zip/Postal Code: _____

*New York residents remit applicable sales taxes.
  Canadian residents remit applicable GST and provincial taxes.   HBACK-JM